Skate School

The world's coolest boarding school!

"I remember now!" Madame Dubois interrupted. "You're the Cinderella of figure skating! Plucked from obscurity at a local ice rink, weren't you? And I suppose that Kristiana von Berne was the fairy godmother, whisking you away to the Alps, teaching you how to skate? You think that going to the Olympics is just like poor Cinders going to the ball!" She cackled with harsh laughter.

Frankie just stared at her, open-mouthed, as the last vestiges of politeness fell away from Madame Dubois. When she'd finally stopped laughing, the woman leaned towards Frankie and spoke slowly and deliberately. "Listen to me carefully, girl. The simple truth is that Sophie LaFleur is a winner. And you're not."

WYNDHAM CITY LIBRARY SERVICE
PO BOX 197
WERRIBEE VIC 3030

Endorsed by the
National Ice Skating Association, UK

"Every budding ice skater will love this book."
Liz Littler, NISA International
Championship Judge

Skate School

Going for Gold

KAY WOODWARD

USBORNE

For Woody, my smashing husband,
who can skate way better than I can

First published in the UK in 2010 by Usborne Publishing Ltd., Usborne House, 83-85 Saffron Hill, London EC1N 8RT, England. www.usborne.com

Copyright © 2010, Chorion Rights Limited, a Chorion company. All rights reserved. Based on an original concept by Jeff Norton.

The right of Kay Woodward to be identified as the author of this work has been asserted by her in accordance with the Copyright, Designs and Patents Act, 1988.

Cover photograph © Graham Taylor. Skater: Stephanie Rigley.

The name Usborne and the devices ♀ ⊕ are Trade Marks of Usborne Publishing Ltd.

All rights reserved. No part of this publication may be reproduced, stored in a retrieval system or transmitted in any form or by any means, electronic, mechanical, photocopying, recording or otherwise without the prior permission of the publisher.

This is a work of fiction. The characters, incidents, and dialogues are products of the author's imagination and are not to be construed as real. Any resemblance to actual events or persons, living or dead, is entirely coincidental.

A CIP catalogue record for this book is available from the British Library.

JFMAMJJAS ND/10   01579/1   ISBN 9780746099285

Printed in Reading, Berkshire, UK.

CHAPTER *One*

"Welcome to the Opening Ceremony of the Winter Olympics!"

The loudspeaker sent sound waves echoing round the crowded tunnel. Every single member of Team GB was here. They stood together proudly, an elite group of world-class snowboarders, cross-country skiers, curlers and – of course – figure skaters, all united by the same magical dream: *to win gold.*

Frankie Wills could hardly believe it. She was

here, at last. She shut her eyes and hugged herself tightly as feelings of delirious excitement swirled through her, swiftly followed by hot panic. And nerves. *So* many nerves.

"Are you okay?" The voice seemed to come from far away.

"Huh?" Frankie wrenched her lids open and found that she was staring dumbstruck into eyes so gorgeously green they could only belong to one person.

Dylan.

"I…er…sorry, I was just a bit overwhelmed by everything," Frankie stammered, pushing messy, dark hair away from her face. She couldn't help being dazzled by his broad smile. Dylan was the best. Well, she thought so, anyway. And if it weren't for the punishing schedule at Skate School – and the fact that Madame von Berne had a complete downer on relationships between her students – they'd have been an item ages ago.

For now, they were just good friends.

Nearby, the crowd roared, reminding Frankie that there were just a few seconds before everything kicked off. Now *wasn't* the time to be staring dreamily at the boy she hoped would be her boyfriend one day.

"Come on," said Alesha, nudging Dylan aside. "We're next!"

Frankie smiled nervously at her. Alesha was the best and most loyal friend a girl could wish for. More at home in head-to-foot black than the red beret, white jacket and black trousers of the Team GB outfit, she still looked fabulous, with her long, jet-black hair and kohl-smudged eyes.

Then Frankie's gaze skittered nervously around the other figure skaters.

Scarlett was admiring her pink lipgloss in a small mirror and casually flicking back glossy blonde hair. Frankie's arch-rival and a wannabe celebrity, she was here to win.

Briefly, Frankie's eyes alighted on Dylan again – she mentally shook herself and her gaze skipped on to Paul. Wiry and thin with dark hair, he was simply great. Apart from one horrible bust-up over the Perfect Pairs competition, they'd always got on. And she so wanted him to do well.

Finally, there were Edward and Anushka – Team GB's hopefuls in the pair skating competition. Tall and elegant, with striking features, cool demeanours and matching sleek, black hair, they were the perfect team.

Frankie could barely believe she belonged with this group of super-talented people. Not so very long ago, she'd been a schoolgirl who loved to skate. But then she'd been discovered by Madame and fast-tracked through Skate School and now she was an ice princess who was here – *really* here – at the Winter Olympics. And she *so* wanted to wow everyone and show them all that the hard work had been worth it. But could she do it? Could she actually win gold for Great Britain…?

"Hey!" said a burly usher, grinning at everyone. "They're waiting for you!"

Scarlett smiled sweetly at the official and then turned to Alesha. "Darling, I know you have problems staying upright on the ice," she said cattily. "Do you think you can manage to walk around an Olympic arena without tripping up?" She gave a tinkling laugh and started to make her way up the ramp.

"Ignore her!" Frankie whispered to Alesha. "She's just trying to wind you up." Gently, she pushed her friend after the other team members and they made their way along the dark, echoing tunnel.

"Good luck, everyone." The cool voice belonged to a petite, dark-haired woman with icy-blue eyes – Madame Kristiana von Berne. To her students, Madame was the single most important person here. The ice princess of her day, she'd fallen at the World Figure Skating Championships and missed gold by a whisker. Her injuries meant that she'd never skated competitively again. But she hadn't left figure skating. Now, she was coaching director for the Team GB figure skating team – and the most glamorous one they'd ever had. She was never seen in anything less than full make-up and stunning clothes. Madame even made the official Olympic outfit look good. She was notoriously bad-tempered and fiercely private too. Last year, she'd allowed Frankie the briefest glimpse of her past, and then refused to speak of it again. All the students wondered what had happened to make her so totally focused on skating. But they had long ago given up hope of ever finding out.

"Let's go," said Madame, a rare smile illuminating her face.

They stepped out into the blindingly bright light.

Wow.

Frankie had never experienced *anything* like this before. The atmosphere was electric, with music and cheering building to a crescendo of noise. And the arena itself looked *amazing* – tier upon tier of seating, crammed with countless spectators who cheered and applauded and wolf-whistled until Frankie felt that if she stopped walking, she'd simply be carried along on an enormous wave of goodwill.

"*Grande-Bretagne! Great Britain!*" cried the commentator.

Frankie just stared. The arena was so vast, you'd need a telescope to see the far side. Plus, of course, this Opening Ceremony would have a TV audience of *millions*. Then the truth hit... *Her dream had come true.* She was the famous figure skater that she'd always wanted to be. And she was about to compete for the biggest prize of them all. It didn't get better than this.

As if by magic, her nerves were replaced by pure adrenalin. "The Olympic Games start here," she murmured. And then, taking a deep breath and filling her lungs with cold air, she stepped forward. Suddenly, she knew that she was going to enjoy herself. A lot.

"Hey," said Paul, "look how they've projected all the flags onto the seating!"

"Cool," said Dylan. He bunched his eyebrows together thoughtfully. "I wonder how they've done that…?"

"Who cares?" said Scarlett. "There are thousands of people here and millions watching us on television around the world. I think we should just wave and smile, don't you?"

For once, Frankie had to admit that the Queen of the Ice – as they all nicknamed Scarlett – was right. As the flag-bearer walked ahead of Team GB, holding the large Union flag up high, she hurried after him.

The Olympic Opening Ceremony was so *big*

that it seemed impossible not to feel shy at first. But as Frankie grew more confident, she began to wave her own miniature flag at the crowds. Soon, she was smiling and waving as madly as the rest of Team GB as the crowd cheered and clapped.

Scarlett held a pink camcorder aloft as she paraded along, flinging her long, golden hair back for the benefit of film crews and photographers.

"What are you doing?" hissed Paul out of the side of his mouth.

"I'm recording an exclusive view of the event, of course," said Scarlett. "They'll need some footage for the TV documentary about my life after this is over."

Everyone laughed – even Madame – as they all moved forward, soaking up the wonderful atmosphere. If it were possible to bottle a moment and keep it for ever, then Frankie would have chosen this one. Camera flashes sparkled in the spectator seating, music blared and the crowds madly applauded the hundreds of athletes who'd travelled to Canada from all around the world.

And Frankie was one of them.

It was an *amazing* feeling.

As the TV cameras swooped by Team GB again, Frankie gave a bashful wave. It was the middle of the night back home in London. But she knew that no matter how late it was, Mum and Dad would be watching. Josh, her sometimes annoying and occasionally cool brother, would be glued to the television too. And her very young twin sisters, Meg and Jess, would catch her on the repeat the next day. She felt a pang as she thought of them all, so far away in London. She wished they were here to watch her skate, but air tickets didn't come cheap and that was that. They'd arranged to Skype each other whenever possible to make up for it.

"Isn't this awesome?" Dylan said, striding along beside her. He caught Frankie's hand and clasped it firmly as they walked onwards. "Is this what it's like being famous, do you think?"

Frankie had a sudden flashback to their hugely embarrassing brush with stardom the year before, when a supposedly secret kiss between herself and Dylan had been shown in living rooms around the world on the reality TV programme, *Stars of the Ice Palace*. She'd hated the attention. But this was very different. Frankie grinned up at Dylan. "Dunno." She shrugged. "But now that I've got over the sheer terror of appearing in front of millions of people, I think I might *actually* be enjoying myself."

As they walked on together, Frankie's thoughts whizzed back to the World Championships, just twelve months earlier. She'd clinched bronze with a stunning performance of her *Swan Lake* program, but Madame had told her bluntly that she needed to do better still for the Olympics. This time, both the short program and the free skate had to be totally, completely and mind-blowingly brilliant, which was a tall order. As if he could read her mind, Dylan gave her hand a quick, comforting squeeze and she smiled up at him gratefully.

"Hey!" said Scarlett.

Stupidly annoyed by her rival butting in, Frankie tried her best not to look bothered as Scarlett snatched Dylan's free hand and caught hold of Paul's hand too. On the other side, Alesha grasped Paul's free hand, while Edward and Anushka joined the end of the line, so all seven of the Team GB skaters were marching along together.

Scarlett held Dylan's hand aloft, to the delight of the crowds. "They know real champions when they see them, don't they?" she murmured under her breath.

Frankie felt a small stab of jealousy. Then, quickly she shrugged it off. Madame was so against figure-skating relationships that she was sure Dylan wouldn't be going out with anyone until the pressure was off, least of all Scarlett. At least, she hoped so.

Tumultuous cheers burst from the grandstands now as the Canadians – the host country were traditionally the last to appear – marched into the arena to join the other teams. The Olympic Opening Ceremony was reaching a crescendo. An intrepid snowboarder whooshed down a ski jump and rocketed through one of the five interlinked circles of the Olympic logo to tumultuous applause. Then the tiny figures of two pop stars – magnified on huge screens – appeared, to sing the theme song of the Games, which signalled the end of the official ceremony…

…and the beginning of the party.

Frankie couldn't stop smiling. This was just the start. How much more amazing would the figure skating be? She couldn't wait to find out.

Bring it on!

CHAPTER *Two*

There was a carnival atmosphere as wild dancing erupted around the arena. Myriad teams began to mingle – the huge Canadian team, the tiny team of one from Colombia, the brightly dressed group of German athletes and so many more besides.

Frankie was swamped by fellow competitors and, in the crush, couldn't help letting go of Dylan's hand. She felt a brief moment of regret, but almost immediately she found herself talking to a curling champion who seemed determined to explain the rules of the baffling sport. And she was so engrossed – much to her surprise, curling actually sounded quite cool – that Frankie didn't spot Dylan until much later. Suddenly, she caught sight of his familiar floppy red hair in the distance and could see that he was shaking hands with a stack of other athletes.

And then Frankie saw Sophie LaFleur – the Canadian figure skater who'd done her best to distract Scarlett before her performance at the Worlds last year and who had gone on to win gold. Sophie waved a teddy bear at someone and her blonde ringlets bobbed up and down as if she were appearing in a shampoo advert. As Frankie watched, Sophie began to weave her way through the crowd, making a beeline for…Dylan. Once she reached him, the two skaters smiled and chatted for what seemed like an eternity.

Frankie forced herself to look away and smiled politely as she shook hands with a Swiss downhill skier who was making a brave comeback after a horrific fall. Dylan could chat to whoever he pleased. But as she stared over the crowd to where

Sophie was now flinging her arms around him and hugging him tightly, she couldn't help feeling a little put out. Because even though Dylan looked a little embarrassed to be monopolized by the Canadian skater like this, Frankie couldn't help thinking that he seemed pleased too.

A little of the Olympic shine began to wear off. Because, deep down, Frankie had hoped to win both gold *and* Dylan's heart.

Jet lag caught up with Frankie the next day. The late night didn't help – they'd gone to a wonderfully glamorous party after the Olympic Opening Ceremony – and neither did the fact that, because of the eight-hour time difference, Frankie kept waking in the small hours of the morning. Today, despite being dog-tired, she was unable to get back to sleep again.

So, it was a little after 6 a.m., so early that the winter sun had yet to rise, that Frankie sat on the apartment's large sofa, staring blearily out of the picture window at the amazing view beyond.

Her mind wandered back to Skate School – the world's coolest and toughest boarding school. This was where Frankie and thirty-odd other students – so many of whom *hadn't* made the grade this time – lived and breathed figure skating, high in the Swiss Alps. They nicknamed the school the Ice Palace, even though it was not a palace at all, just a collection of scattered buildings and an ice rink. But it *was* a magical place where dreams were made.

The question was, did Frankie have what it took to make those dreams come true? She was only sixteen and yet she was taking part in the biggest sporting event in the world. In the cold dawn light, it suddenly seemed so much scarier and more serious than it had the night before...

"Coffee?" mumbled Alesha, appearing from their bedroom and thankfully interrupting Frankie's gloomy thoughts.

"Yeah," said Frankie.

Alesha collapsed onto the sofa beside her. "I'll get it in a minute," she said. "I'm too tired to move."

"It's okay," said Frankie, with a wonky grin. "I'm probably too tired to drink it."

They both dissolved into mildly hysterical giggles before returning their weary gazes to the sleeping city outside.

"Beautiful, isn't it?" said Alesha.

Frankie nodded wordlessly. The dark Vancouver skyline was dominated by tower blocks twinkling with multicoloured lights. And she could just see glimpses of the harbour beyond. The day before the Olympic Opening Ceremony, they'd visited the magnificent park on the headland that was teeming with wildlife. It was just like being in the countryside and hard to imagine that 600,000 people lived just next door. Then, Scarlett had dragged them to the shops, declaring that a girl couldn't live on squirrel-spotting alone, and Frankie had to admit that the fantastic boutiques and enormous stores weren't bad either.

"Nearly as good as New York City," Scarlett had grudgingly admitted, weighed down by bulging shopping bags.

Frankie had decided that sometime, ideally when she *wasn't* competing in the most important figure-skating competition in the world, she'd love to come back here to explore, just so that she could appreciate the amazing Canadian city properly.

"Hey," said Alesha, stretching lazily. "We're not expected to practise today, are we? Only I don't think I can. I'm just *too* tired." She yawned.

"It's a rest day," replied Frankie, "which is why it's even more annoying that I'm awake this early." She gave a short laugh. "I don't know what time Scarlett got in last night, but she was snoring like a warthog just now. I don't know how Anushka stands it."

"Earplugs," said Alesha with a grin. "I saw Scarlett chatting to a Canadian ice hockey player for ages at the party," she added. "No doubt we'll have to listen to her boasting about her new conquest later." She got to her feet. "I think I can summon the energy to switch the kettle on now," she added. "Still fancy a cuppa?"

"Yes, please," replied Frankie. She followed Alesha to the small kitchenette area of the spacious apartment that they were sharing with Scarlett and Anushka during their stay in the Olympic Village. There were two bedrooms – one with bunk beds, and a larger twin room that Scarlett had had no hesitation in snaffling for herself and Anushka as soon as they'd arrived.

The boys were staying in another apartment with a couple of snowboarders. "There is something that I *would* like to do," said Frankie thoughtfully. "I'd like to check out the figure-skating venue." She knew it was just an ice rink – an Olympic-sized one, naturally – but she needed to prepare mentally for the event. And sussing out the venue was part of that process.

"That's a *great* idea," said Alesha, spooning out instant coffee. "As long as you don't make me actually skate, that is. I don't think I could land a bunny hop today." She poured boiling water into two large mugs and added milk before handing a mug to Frankie. "I found these, too," she added, producing a packet of croissants. "Want one?"

"Mmm..." said Frankie, a wave of hunger washing over her. She bit into the slightly stale croissant and sighed happily. "Suddenly, I'm feeling a whole lot better," she said.

"Me too," agreed Alesha. "Give me five minutes to shower and then I'm up for anything."

* * *

The ice rink was quite the most magical place that Frankie had ever seen. Ever. Madison Square Garden – where she'd skated at the Worlds – had been good, but this was better still. She and Alesha watched as the Zamboni machine made its slow, majestic way around the rink, leaving perfect stripes of smooth ice in its wake. The figure-skating competitions didn't start for another couple of days, but in the meantime it was being used for the speed skating events. And after the figure-skating medals had been awarded, it would become the venue for the final event of the Winter Olympics – the ice-hockey competition.

"Ooh." Frankie leaned against the barrier, her breath misting the air. Suddenly, there was nothing in the world she'd rather be doing than relaxing into long, swooping back crossovers around the perimeter of the rink, followed by a layback spin – the world whizzing faster and faster as she reached back, one leg stretched behind her as she leaned into the spin. She knew that it would feel so good to get back on the ice, especially after the long, cramped flight and the excitement of the Opening Ceremony.

"Earth calling Frankie!" said Alesha. Her eyes twinkled merrily. "You're aching to get out there, aren't you?"

Frankie grinned as she came back down to earth with a thud. There was nothing she'd like better… but she knew that they were restricted to the official practice sessions. "I've got a better idea," she said. "Let's grab something else to eat. I don't know what it is about jet lag, but I'm *starving* today."

It didn't take a great deal of investigating to track down a coffee shop in the stadium and soon Frankie and Alesha were enjoying iced doughnuts and steaming hot chocolate as they stared out across the rink.

"If I tell you something, swear you won't tell another soul?" Alesha mumbled through a mouthful of doughnut. "Not even Dylan?"

"Er…yes," said Frankie, wondering what on earth could be the matter. This sounded serious.

Alesha chewed her lip for a few seconds, before blurting it out. "I'm totally bricking it," she said.

"Oh, is that *all*?" Frankie said, letting out a sigh of relief. "I'm scared *too*. I thought you were going to tell me something really awful, like you'd developed an allergy to ice or something."

"Yes, but you're *good*," Alesha persisted. "One of the newspapers called you the *Ice Princess* last week. You've got nothing to worry about."

Privately, Frankie disagreed with this. She had *everything* to worry about: whether she could land the triple toe-loop on her blade and not her behind; whether her programs were too complex or – even worse – not complex enough; whether Dylan and Sophie LaFleur were about to become an item… The list went on and on.

"I can't believe I've made it this far, and I'm not sure Madame can either," said Alesha, staring gloomily into her cup. "And I *am* here, which is great, but I don't know if I'm actually going to be able to hold it together on the ice. What if I'm a total disaster?" By now, her eyes were swimming with unshed tears.

"Oh, Alesha!" said Frankie softly. "Everything will be *fine*." But she knew why her best friend was nervous. Alesha skated like a demon – but only *sometimes*. And then, all too often, a silly mistake would turn a wildly brilliant routine into a complete disaster. Luckily, the British Olympic Association and Madame had decided to take a risk on her. The question was – would that risk pay off? Frankie *really* hoped so. But rather than let Alesha dwell on the challenge ahead, she decided to change the subject. "What do you reckon to Scarlett's chances?" she asked.

"If she stops shopping long enough to compete, then who knows?" said Alesha. "Technically, she's wonderful. But her routine lacks...a certain...I don't know...emotion? I admire her skill, but her performances don't whisk me away to another world – not like *yours* do."

"Er...right," said Frankie, her cheeks reddening. She ignored the compliment and ploughed on. "She's determined to win, you know. This time, I don't think anyone can stop her grabbing the gold with both hands."

Alesha snorted, before moving swiftly on to Olga Krugalov, another of the female competitors.

The Russian star was one to watch – all the sports pundits said so. But Alesha had some new gossip. "I've heard that she's been devoting a lot more time to modelling than she has to figure skating lately," she told Frankie. "Olga's coach is Tatiana Dubrovich. You know, one of Madame's rivals from back in the 1980s? I've heard that she's not happy about it."

Frankie grimaced. She and all of the other members of Team GB knew just what it was like to be at the receiving end of a coach's wrath. Madame von Berne's acid tongue was legendary. But Frankie also couldn't work out why someone would want to risk Olympic dreams in exchange for a few photos in a magazine. She wanted to win so badly it hurt.

"Hey, *there* you are!"

Startled out of her reverie, Frankie looked up and spotted the one person guaranteed to make her feel good: Dylan. He strode around the rink towards them, Scarlett and Paul close behind.

"I'm so glad we've found you," Dylan said, stopping directly in front of Frankie and towering above her. "Paul's really excited about something but he's refusing to spill the beans until he has everyone together."

Scarlett stood with her hands on her hips and tutted. "I don't even really care what it is, anyway."

"Obviously," said Alesha, raising her eyebrows.

Paul plonked himself down on the seat beside Frankie, looking as if he'd already won a gold medal. "Listen to *this*," he said.

CHAPTER *Three*

Paul looked from Frankie to Alesha, Scarlett and Dylan in turn. "Are you ready for me to blow you away with the best idea *ever*…?"

Alesha rolled her eyes.

"Oh, just spit it out," said Scarlett, brushing back her long golden hair with elegant, manicured fingers. "I haven't got all day."

Paul ignored her. "So this is it: why don't we all go and watch the men's snowboard cross event?" he said. "All we need to do is catch the shuttle bus up to the mountains and then we can watch the greatest show on earth." He grinned. "Sorry, that's the figure skating. The *second* greatest show on earth."

"What about Edward and Anushka?" said Frankie. "What are they doing?"

"Talking tactics," said Paul. "*Boring.*"

"I'm not sure..." Frankie murmured, feeling uneasy.

Scarlett tutted. "Why not?" she asked. "I think it's a fabulous plan."

"Madame will be furious if we go off without permission," said Frankie. "And what about the big meal tonight?"

"We'll be back in plenty of time for dinner." Paul smiled.

Frankie bit her lip.

The Zamboni machine whooshed past on the other side of the barrier, smoothing and polishing the ice in great shiny arcs and making conversation impossible for a few seconds. Frankie couldn't help but feel nervous. She was so focused on the upcoming figure-skating competition that it felt wrong even to be *thinking* about watching the other

Olympic events. But, on the other hand, the snowboard cross sounded very tempting…

"So?" said Paul. "How about it? We'd be fools not to go."

Scarlett pursed her glossy pink lips while she examined her fingernails.

"I'm in," said Dylan, with a lopsided grin. "I've only tried snowboarding once and I was totally rubbish, but I'm going to work out how to do it one day. It'd be great to watch the experts."

"Oh, I agree," Scarlett said quickly. "I'm already a world-class skier, but if I tried, I know that I'd be brilliant at snowboarding too. And I just adore snowboard chic. It's *so* cool."

Alesha sniggered.

"I don't know what you're laughing at," sneered Scarlett. "All you ever wear is black. You wouldn't know chic if it slapped you round the face with a wet fish—"

"Okay!" interrupted Frankie, her mind made up. Jet lag, rest, relaxation and even precious sleep could wait. "If you'll all please just *stop bickering* then I'm in, all right?"

"Whatever," drawled Scarlett, rolling her eyes.

Did the blonde-haired Queen of the Ice look disappointed that her skating rival would be going too? Frankie wasn't sure. She just hoped that she could bag a seat next to Dylan on the bus, because since they'd arrived here, she seemed to have spent almost zero time with him.

But it wasn't to be.

As soon as they arrived at the bus stop, Sophie LaFleur rushed over to Dylan in a cloud of whiffy perfume. "Dylan!" she cried. The Canadian girl was dressed in her offical Olympic outfit like the rest of them. She wore a hooded top – red with black and white sleeves – and black trousers. Blonde ringlets curled from beneath her totally stylish red-and-white skullcap. But her thin, sharp face was exactly as Frankie remembered it from the World Figure Skating Championships the year before. And from the moment she muscled into the queue and caught Dylan by the elbow, one thing was perfectly clear. Sophie was going to allow only one person to sit next to Dylan. And that was Sophie herself.

* * *

"Ooh…" sighed Frankie as the bus zigzagged left and right up the mountain road, the view becoming more magnificent with every bend. She must have been mad to consider missing out on this trip. But she couldn't help looking enviously towards Dylan and Sophie. They were sitting together near the front of the bus – both staring out at the stunning view.

"Don't let her get to you," whispered Alesha. "I told you before. She's just trying to wind you up by shoehorning herself into our group. I bet she's heard about your routine and she's scared that you're going to beat her."

"Yeah, right…" said Frankie. But she couldn't help feeling left out. It wasn't as if Dylan had tried very hard to sit with Frankie instead. On the contrary, he seemed thrilled by the other girl's attention.

"We'll be there soon," said Paul, who was in the seat behind Frankie, sitting next to a glowering Scarlett. "I think the snowboard cross qualifying session kicks off at 2.30, so we'll be in plenty of time to grab a burger or something first. I'm sure we can get a pass into the VIP area."

"Oh?" said Scarlett, brightening instantly. "Well, thank goodness for that."

"Would you look at *that*?" Dylan called back over his shoulder. He pointed out of the window, almost knocking off Sophie's hat, as the bus slowed and the gondola terminal loomed large.

"I think this is where we get off," said Paul.

Frankie rubbed condensation off the bus window with her sleeve and gazed at the view. She didn't know which was more impressive – the craggy mountainsides that climbed steeply upwards or the sheer numbers of spectators jostling to get inside the gondola terminal. A *lot* of people wanted to watch the snowboard cross. She hurried after the others, suddenly keen to find out what all the fuss was about.

Detaching himself from Sophie's side at last, Dylan pushed through the crowds and joined them in the packed gondola. Much to Frankie's delight, he flung an arm around her shoulder and then spent the twenty-minute journey up into the mountains boring them with technical facts about the cable-car system.

"Will someone please shut him up?" muttered Alesha, who didn't like heights at all. "I don't *want* to know where they join the never-ending cable…"

Obligingly, Dylan switched to the rules of snowboard cross instead. "It's seriously awesome," he said, squeezing Frankie's hand as he spoke.

She blushed quickly, thrilled that Dylan was paying her some attention at last. "Four snowboarders race each other down a course that can be described as 'challenging' at best and 'totally mad' at worst. There are half-pipes and a whole load of jumps," he said. "First two to get to the finishing line are through to the next round. Hey, there's *ski* cross too," Dylan added, with a devilish glint in his eye. "Same course, but competitors have two planks on their feet rather than one. Seeing as you're such an expert skier, Scarlett, why don't you try it sometime?"

Scarlett smiled at him, her eyes narrowed. "Oh, I'm going to concentrate on winning a gold medal at figure skating first," she said sweetly. "I don't want to show off."

"That'll be the day," Alesha muttered to her knees, too scared to look out of the window at the magnificent view.

A moment later, the gondola entered the terminal building and swung round a bend, its doors sliding open to give the passengers plenty of time to step out before collecting the few passengers on their journey back down to the valley below.

Frankie tapped Alesha on the shoulder. "You can relax now," she said softly. "We're here."

CHAPTER *Four*

As she stepped outside the gondola station into the winter sunshine, Frankie took a deep gulp of mountain air and gasped as the bitter cold flooded her lungs.

"Brrr!" she shivered, not just with cold, but with excitement too. Sliding on her sunglasses to shield her eyes from the harsh glare of the brilliantly white snow, she looked around curiously. So *this* was what an Olympic resort looked like. Crowds of spectators dressed in waterproof, windproof and snowproof performance clothing of every imaginable colour milled about, counting down the minutes to the beginning of today's event.

"I think it's this way," said Paul, heading towards the VIP area.

"*Au revoir*, Dylan!" sang Sophie LaFleur, stepping out of the next gondola to arrive. She detached herself from a group of burly Canadian ice hockey players and planted one…two…*three* kisses on Dylan's reddening cheeks. "See you later, *cheri*." Tilting her head coyly, she smiled at him from beneath perfectly mascaraed lashes before returning to her teammates – but not before she'd flung a dark look in Frankie's direction.

Recoiling from the other girl's unfriendly stare, Frankie remembered how annoyed she'd been when Sophie LaFleur had singled out Scarlett for her nastiness at last year's Worlds. Then, she had felt put out that Sophie didn't rate Frankie enough of a rival to spend time trying to put her off before her performance. It seemed that Sophie had changed her mind. But were Sophie and Frankie just rivals for gold…or for Dylan too?

Frankie had no idea. But, determined to put the unpleasant episode out of her mind, she wriggled stiff fingers into her fleece-lined mittens and hurried after Dylan and the others. She wasn't about to let Sophie LaFleur ruin a once-in-a-lifetime experience.

The spectators waited impatiently for the beeps that would signal the start of the heats. Frankie craned her head to the right, just able to make out the opening gates where the snowboarders would start the race. She and the others had been waiting for an hour now and their anticipation had grown to epic proportions. The crowd shuffled restlessly around them, the air so charged with energy that Frankie could almost feel it buzzing.

Beep beep beep!

The race began and the competitors swooshed into action.

"Woo!" cried Alesha as the four super-elite snowboarders launched themselves off the lip of the first jump and sailed into the air, landing with varying degrees of success on the slope below. One snowboarder somersaulted out of the competition, while another caught an edge and looked as if he might be going the same way, saving himself at the last moment. The massive crowd cheered its approval as the remaining three competitors headed for the deadly half-pipe, before swooping round the great curve in the course.

"Isn't this awesome?" said Paul, turning to the others and grinning broadly. "I *knew* you'd all love it."

"I *do*," said Scarlett, staring enviously after the snowboarders as they hurtled downhill and out of sight. "I'm going to take lessons as soon as I've won gold in the figure skating. I'll need a new challenge after that."

Alesha rolled her eyes and Frankie forced herself to look down in case she giggled. She no longer took the other girl's comments seriously. Scarlett was a big-head and that was that.

The next hour flew by, each successive heat more exciting than the last. Frankie was having the best time – until she caught sight of her watch and her stomach clenched anxiously.

"Hey, guys," she said. "It's nearly four o'clock. Do you think we should be making a move? If we head for the gondola now, we'll miss the rush."

"But we'll miss the final too," Paul said, wearing his most pleading smile. "Go on, it's hardly got going… And you *know* that you want to stay really. It'd be a shame to come all this way and then miss the best bit of the entire competition."

"Oh, come on, Goody-Two-Skates," Scarlett said in a sugar-coated voice that barely hid the contempt beneath. "I'm sure Madame would like us to have fun on our rest day, right?"

"I don't know…" sighed Frankie. She really didn't want to make Madame mad, but on the other hand, it was very tempting to stay and join in the fun. "Just half an hour more?" she said. "That should give us long enough to get back in plenty of time before dinner."

"Sounds good to me," said Dylan, with a wink at Frankie.

"Yeah," agreed Alesha. "Any longer than that and I'll turn into a block of ice."

Frankie breathed a sigh of relief. After her previous clashes with Madame, there was no way she wanted to be late. But half an hour came and went and the competition went on. An hour later, the competitors were still plummeting down the roller coaster course to rapturous applause. But Frankie wasn't enjoying it any more. How long would it be before the final heat? She was sure it wouldn't be happening any time soon. And meanwhile, the seconds were ticking away. Now it was just two hours until dinner.

Feeling like the biggest party pooper in town, Frankie tried yet again to hurry the others. "We really should be going now," she said.

"Oh, will you just give it a rest?" said Scarlett. "We'd be having a great time here if you weren't bleating on and on like a distressed sheep."

"Hey, I've got an idea," said Dylan. "I'll give Madame a call and warn her that we're going to be late, okay? Then she won't be worrying about us."

"All right…" Frankie said reluctantly. But she wasn't happy. And when Dylan pocketed his mobile with a shrug, unable to get through to the coaching director but promising to try again in a few minutes, she felt unhappier still. There was nothing she could do about it though. She'd told Mum and Dad that she'd stay with the others rather than exploring on her own. So she was stuck here until everyone else wanted to leave.

Despite everything, the men's snowboard cross final was nothing short of wonderful and, apart from an underlying feeling of worry, Frankie loved every adrenalin-fuelled second. The euphoria of the event spilled over into the medal ceremony, which was arranged with speedy efficiency. Breck Dexter, the blond Canadian who'd been the firm favourite to win, accepted his gold medal with cool nonchalance, nodding in a laid-back manner at the crowd.

Frankie was pushed forward by the delighted spectators, all keen to get a closer look at the new gold medallist. Carried away by it all, she joined in the deafening cheers for the athletes, trying to imagine what it must feel like to be on the Olympic winners' podium and wishing so hard that she'd get the chance to find out. She saw that Breck was grinning lazily in her direction and clapped louder, wondering who he was looking at. With a jolt, she realized that it was...*her*.

And then things got seriously weird.

Breck Dexter winked.

CHAPTER *Five*

Apart from turning beetroot-red, Frankie didn't know *what* to do after the bizarre wink. She looked guiltily towards Dylan and noticed with relief that he wasn't looking at her or the medal winners. Instead, he was shouting into his mobile phone, apparently in an effort to make the person at the other end of the line hear over the loud cheering. Good. That meant that he hadn't seen a thing.

Frankie risked a covert glance at Breck. But he was now sitting on the shoulders of his teammates and holding his gold medal aloft, to the delight of the many Canadian supporters. He was no longer looking in Frankie's direction. Had she just imagined the wink?

"Hey, good news!" cried Dylan, catching Frankie in an unexpected hug. "That was Madame von Berne on the phone. I told her where we were and while I can't say that she sounded totally delighted that we'd be late for dinner, she didn't give me a roasting either. Told me that we should come back as soon as we can and that we'd discuss it later." He grinned. "So we're off the hook!"

"Oh, er…right," said Frankie, unsure whether to feel pleased or not. For her, the immediate worry of being late for dinner had now been replaced with the vaguely troubling feeling that they'd be facing the music whenever they *did* get back. "We should hurry then," she said.

"Frankie's right," Alesha said. "Shall we get going?"

Paul shrugged. "You can try," he said reasonably. "But there's probably no point. Have you seen the queues?" He pointed back towards the centre of the resort, where long lines of people snaked away from the gondola terminal building. It was the only way down the mountain and suddenly there were a lot of people who wanted to get home.

"Great…" Frankie's heart sank. The queues were growing longer and longer as she watched. It looked like they were going to be stuck up here for *hours*. She gazed around at the stunning view and saw that the sun was just setting over the mountains. Already, the sky was streaked with pink and purple. Soon, it would be night-time and the temperature would plummet.

"Cheer up," said Alesha. "It could be worse. We could be trapped at altitude without a band to entertain us." She gestured back towards the snowboard cross track. "Look!"

Despite her anxiety, Frankie couldn't help laughing. Where, just a few moments ago, the medal winners had been celebrating their success, the podium was now occupied by a group of musicians busy tuning their guitars.

"Huh," said Scarlett. "As if we're even going to *hear* them."

Twangggggg!

The thrum of an electric chord reverberated through a nearby speaker.

"Oh," said Scarlett.

The band had managed to plug themselves into the official PA system. A sea of heads turned towards the musicians. Meanwhile, the relentless flow of spectators towards the gondolas began to slow. *"Are you ready to party?"* cried the lead guitarist.

The crowd roared its approval and the band responded by exploding into life with their version of the Olympic song that was at the top of the music downloads this week.

For a moment, Frankie knew just what it must feel like to be a hamster on a wheel, going round and round and never getting anywhere. Because no matter how hard she tried to get the others to come back with her to the Olympic Village – and avoid Madame's wrath – she just couldn't manage it. Abruptly, she decided to quit trying and to enjoy the music instead.

"Let's dance!" she said to Dylan.

A broad smile lit up Dylan's freckly face as he

wrapped his arms around Frankie and swung her off her feet. "I thought you'd never ask," he whispered.

Soon, Frankie was having the best time. Worries about Madame melted away like snow in springtime. The band was seriously good. The guitarists played a string of hits, each one funkier than the last. Frankie danced with Dylan and when a surge in the crowd flung them apart, she shrugged helplessly at him and danced with Alesha instead.

"Having fun?" Frankie cried to her best friend.

Alesha, who was swaying soulfully along to the music, swept messy dark hair from her eyes and nodded. "It's not my sort of thing," she said. "Bit too rock and pop and not enough drum and bass for my taste. But it'll do." She grinned at Frankie and then her eyes slid left as she looked over her friend's shoulder. "I think someone's looking for you," she added.

Frankie spun round wearing her biggest smile, expecting to see Dylan – but coming face-to-face instead with none other than the medal winner, Breck Dexter. "Oh," she said. "Er…hi.

Congratulations on the…er…gold." She was mega-confused. What did Breck *want*?

"How are *you* doing?" said Breck, who was apparently oblivious to her puzzled expression. His artfully tousled surf-dude hairdo made him look as if he'd just stepped off a beach rather than a winners' podium. But the gold medal that glinted under the spotlights proved otherwise.

"Er, well…um…fine, thanks." Frankie could feel herself blushing just as hotly as when he'd winked at her earlier. "Are you getting me mixed up with someone else?" she asked the Canadian shyly. "Only, I don't think we've actually met."

"Sorry," said Breck, not sounding in the least apologetic. "It's just that I've seen you so often on YouTube that I think I know you already. You starred in that cute TV show about figure skaters, right? And weren't you in the famous clip from the Rockefeller ice rink?"

Frankie nodded. When the video of Dylan and herself giving an impromptu performance had been posted on the internet by a fan, they'd become overnight sensations. But even so, she wasn't used to Olympic medal winners showering her with attention like this. Though she had to admit that it wasn't unpleasant. "That's right," she said quickly. "I skated with Dylan—"

"Yeah, yeah," Breck interrupted with a casual wave of his hand. "Whatever. You skated *really* well."

"Oh," said Frankie awkwardly. "Right." Suddenly eager to escape, her gaze flitted around the crowd, searching for someone that might rescue her. But Dylan was near the band now, with Paul. And Alesha had vanished. The only person she saw was Scarlett, who arched an eyebrow at Frankie and then pointedly turned away. Clearly, she would be no help.

"You're a brilliant figure skater, you know," Breck was saying. "Those triple whatever-you-call-them jumps are awesome. And the spins where you lean back…"

"Layback spins?" Frankie said.

"Yeah…layback spins," agreed Breck, nodding in slow motion. "They make me feel dizzy just watching." He spoke so smoothly and confidently, and said such amazingly complimentary things, that even though she knew she probably shouldn't, Frankie couldn't help warming to him. Before she knew it, Breck had grabbed her hand and was pulling her through the crowd. "Come and meet my snowboarding buddies," he drawled, stopping to sign someone's T-shirt on the way.

"Hey, dudes!" called Breck to a bunch of impossibly cool snowboarders. He grasped Frankie by the shoulders and pushed her forward as they approached. "Frankie, meet the guys. Guys, meet Frankie. She's *awesome*."

"Er…well, I'm not—" began Frankie. But no one seemed to hear her. They were all listening to Breck, as he spoke over her, telling his friends just what a wonderful skater she was and how he was going to be cheering her on at the ice rink every time she skated. Desperately, Frankie tried to butt in, but Breck simply put his arm around her and carried on talking. Frankie felt increasingly uncomfortable. It seemed so much darker now; it really was getting late.

And then it was much, much too late, because

the one person in the world who Frankie didn't want to see her being hugged by another guy was standing just a couple of metres away, staring right at her.

Dylan.

His lips set in a straight line, he turned and walked swiftly away.

"Hey," stammered Frankie, tearing herself out of Breck's grip. "Sorry, I've got to go," she said to his startled face, before hurrying into the crowd after Dylan. He couldn't be *jealous*, could he? But there was no *reason* to be jealous. "Wait!" she called, desperate to explain.

But if Dylan could hear her, he wasn't letting on. He walked on as if she hadn't spoken.

Frankie's shoulders slumped. This *couldn't* be happening. For the millionth time, she regretted coming to watch the stupid snowboard cross at all. Everything would have been fine if she'd stayed in the Olympic Village. And now, because of some silly misunderstanding, Dylan was mad at her. Frankie couldn't help feeling responsible. She'd been enjoying the attention – it had been so lovely to have an Olympic medallist boasting about her. But the warm glow had been short-lived. Miserably, she pushed through the crowd, trying to find Dylan, but colliding instead with Scarlett.

For once, her rival looked delighted to see her. "Frankie!" she said. "Isn't this just the best party ever?"

Frankie shrugged. "Not really," she said. "I'd just like to go home now."

"Oh, don't be a spoilsport!" Scarlett laughed, grooving to the music. She grabbed Frankie's hand and spun her round. Frankie tried to get past her. She *had* to find Dylan. But Scarlett just kept getting in the way. "The music's so cool," shouted Scarlett. "And everyone's having such a great time... especially *Dylan*." Her face wreathed in smiles, she pointed to the far side of the crowd. "Look, Frankie. Doesn't *he* look as if he's enjoying himself?"

Something told Frankie that she wasn't going to like what she saw. And she didn't. There, on the other side of the partying crowd was Dylan...with Sophie LaFleur. Frankie stared at them in horror. A terrible day had just got a whole lot worse.

"Don't they look like they're getting on?" Scarlett went on. Her running commentary was relentless, as if she were really enjoying this. "Sophie's just hugging him because she likes him. There's really nothing between them. And the fact she's holding his hand probably means nothing. I wouldn't worry about it. Well, not unless she kisses him, that is." Scarlett paused. "Oh, Frankie. Did you see that? She *kissed* him!" Not even bothering to hide her glee, Scarlett burst into peals of delighted laughter.

The worst thing was, every single thing that Scarlett had said was true. Dylan and Sophie were hugging *and* they were holding hands. And Sophie *had* kissed him as if they were more than just friends.

Frankie felt as if she'd been punched. And suddenly, she couldn't stand it for a second longer. Hastily brushing away quick tears, she pushed her way through the crowd. She was fed up of waiting for the others. Suddenly, she wasn't bothered if anyone came with her or not.

She was going back to the Olympic Village.

And she was going back right now.

CHAPTER *Six*

Frankie raced through the Olympic resort as if wolves were chasing after her, dodging burger vans and TV-camera operators and doing her best not to skid on the hard-packed snow underfoot. She saw with relief that the gondola terminal was now deserted. Good. There would be no one to witness the tears that were coursing down her cheeks.

As the gondola slowed and swung round the corner, its doors sliding open, Frankie hurried inside, grateful that she'd have at least twenty minutes to compose herself while the cable car made its leisurely way down the mountain. She turned to stare out of the large window at the darkening mountains. She was alone, at last.

And then, just before the gondola doors closed, Frankie heard brisk footsteps. The gondola shook slightly as someone else stepped on board. Her heart sank.

"Well, hello!" It was a woman's voice, deep and vaguely accented.

Quickly brushing away tears, Frankie turned to face her. The newcomer was familiar, but she couldn't place her.

The woman didn't leave Frankie guessing for long. "Madame Valentine Dubois," she said.

Of course... This was Sophie LaFleur's coach. They'd never spoken, but Frankie remembered seeing her at the Worlds last year, where her protégée had won gold to Frankie's bronze. And now she was coming over to Frankie and extending a hand towards her. Obediently, Frankie shook it, noticing that Madame Dubois wore tan leather gloves. They were incredibly stylish, like the rest of her, and made Frankie's own mittens look totally childlike. Instead of the usual hi-tech snow gear, the woman was clad in a floor-length white wool coat, a black scarf and grey fur Cossack hat. She reminded Frankie a little of Madame von Berne.

"Nice to meet you," muttered Frankie, with what she hoped was finality. She turned back to the window, preparing to concentrate on the towering pine trees that lined the route back down the mountainside. Surely Madame Dubois had no interest in someone like her.

Frankie was wrong.

"So…" began the Canadian coach.

Reluctantly, Frankie looked back and watched as the woman plucked a lipstick from her handbag and began casually applying dark red colour to her thin lips. "You must be very excited about the Olympic Games, yes?"

"Er…yes," said Frankie, frowning and wondering if the woman was stupid. Who wouldn't be excited at such an opportunity?

"I don't expect you to tell me what elements you'll be performing in your programs, of course," said the woman, with a polite laugh. "You must be keeping that *very* secret. Don't want to give away clues to the opposition, right?"

"Right…" agreed Frankie, wondering what the coach was driving at. She was perfectly correct. There was no way any figure skater would be sharing any information at all about either of their programs. Madame Dubois must know that. "Anyway…" She smiled politely before turning back to the view and hoping that the woman got the message. Frankie wasn't in the mood for talking to *anyone* right now – and least of all to her rival's coach.

For a few moments, there was silence and Frankie stared doggedly out of the window at the gathering darkness. The sun had long gone and now even the beautiful sunset colours were fading too. Outside, tall, shadowy fir trees streamed past, their branches laden with last night's heavy fall of snow. Harsh lights illuminated the interior of the gondola and were mirrored in the large windows, along with Frankie's sad face. She stared disconsolately at her reflection. Over her shoulder, she could also see

Madame Dubois, pretending to examine the contents of her handbag.

"We're looking forward to the free program, of course," said Madame Dubois pleasantly, as if they were in the middle of a cosy, fireside chat.

Again, Frankie turned to face her. Clearly, she wasn't going to be allowed to mope on her own. "Mmm," she replied, non-committally.

"It's a chance to let yourself go, don't you think?" said Madame Dubois, her eyes glittering. "I mean, obviously, short programs are important too, but I'm sure you can skate yours in your sleep by now. It's the free programs that audiences love. They're just so exhilarating, aren't they? Full of energy and risk and *dazzle*."

Frankie shrugged. Right now, she was so upset about Dylan that she couldn't bring herself to think about figure skating. She flashed back to his hurt, angry expression and bit her lip as it began to tremble once more. She *couldn't* lose it again.

"How's *your* free program, Frankie?" Madame Dubois went on. She didn't wait for an answer. "Is it good enough? You're not as experienced as some of the others – Sophie, for example. When the competition's so stiff, you *must* be nervous that you'll mess up..." Frankie had the sudden impression that the coach was just toying with her like a lion toys with prey...before going in for the kill. "Sophie's a brilliant skater, Frankie. Are you worried that beside her, you'll look like a *beginner*...?"

And there it was, the jibe that the other woman had been storing up for the entire cable-car journey. Frankie couldn't help thinking that it would have been less painful if Madame Dubois had simply poked her in the eye. She peered out of the window and saw that the lights in the valley were much nearer now. But there was still some way to go. Frankie stared at the patterned metal floor of the gondola, willing the mechanism to go faster and whizz her down to the valley floor before the coach could hurl any more insults in her direction. Deep down, she knew that the coach was trying to unsettle her, but much of what she'd said was the truth. Frankie *did* have doubts about her own ability. And she *was* worried that she wouldn't be as good as Sophie. She didn't want to *fail*.

"The thing is, my dear," the coach said sweetly. "You just don't stand a chance. This is your first Olympics. It's natural that you wouldn't be used to the stresses and strains of the international figure-skating circuit. The pressure to do well…the intense competition… It's tougher than you can even begin to imagine."

As Madame Dubois smiled, Frankie noticed the tiny streaks of red that feathered outwards from her lipstick into the fine wrinkles around her mouth. She looked like someone who had spent much of her life pursing her lips.

"Sophie, on the other hand…" continued the coach. "Well, Sophie is a total star. She's been skating since the age of five. She's trained harder and longer than you can imagine and she has countless medals to show for it. She's *earned* her place at the Olympics."

Frankie blinked, unable to believe that someone could say such horrible things to her. She was used to Scarlett poking fun, but this woman made Scarlett look like an amateur. This woman was *mean*.

"I've as much right to be here as anyone!" snapped Frankie, breaking her silence at last. "Just because Sophie has been training since she was five and I—"

"I remember now!" Madame Dubois interrupted. "You're the Cinderella of figure skating! Plucked from obscurity at a local ice rink, weren't you? And I suppose that Kristiana von Berne was the fairy godmother, whisking you away to the Alps, teaching you how to skate? *You* think that going to the Olympics is just like poor Cinders going to the ball!" She cackled with harsh laughter.

Frankie just stared at her, open-mouthed, as the last vestiges of politeness fell away from Madame Dubois. When she'd finally stopped laughing, the woman leaned towards Frankie and spoke slowly and deliberately. "Listen to me carefully, girl. The simple truth is that Sophie LaFleur is a winner. And you're not."

"You're wrong," muttered Frankie. Anger flooded through her and she blinked back hot tears as she stared defiantly into the coach's narrowed eyes. "I've as much chance as *anyone*."

For a few seconds, neither looked away. And then, suddenly, the spell was broken as the gondola jerked very slightly, lifting off the main cable mechanism and onto the slower track on which it travelled into the terminal building.

Madame Dubois gracefully rose to her feet and, ignoring Frankie, shrugged her handbag onto her shoulder and smoothed down her elegant coat. She turned and waited in front of the doors. Then, just as they slid open, the woman looked back. "Sophie will win gold," she said. "Go home, Frankie. There's nothing for you here." The coached smiled and then stepped out of the gondola, leaving the terminal building without a backward glance.

Totally frozen to the spot, Frankie stared in disbelief as Madame Valentine Dubois marched towards a waiting limousine. She was only jerked out of her reverie when she saw that unless she hurried, the doors would close once more and she'd be whisked back up the mountain. And that was the last place on earth she wanted to go. Quickly, Frankie hopped out of the gondola and headed for the bus stop. It would be ages before she reached the Olympic Village and she had *plenty* to think about on the return trip.

Suddenly, being late for dinner was the least of her troubles.

CHAPTER *Seven*

Frankie glided forward, her left foot sliding sleekly over the ice and her right leg stretched behind her. The ice was like silk, so smooth that she could barely feel it beneath her blade. Effortlessly, she changed direction and swooped backwards, leaping into a dazzling triple Axel, the rotations tight and controlled and the landing nothing short of perfect.

A single spotlight followed Frankie around the ice, pausing as she spun and sweeping along with her as she sped around the perimeter of the rink with blade-perfect crossovers, her arms held wide. Everything beyond the circle of light was velvety darkness. There was no music.

Happiness coursed through Frankie as she flung herself into a stunning combination of jumps... triple toe-loop, double loop and a triple Salchow so high that she almost felt as if she were flying. Landing soundlessly, she danced across the middle of the rink with footwork that was neat, precise and – like the rest of her skating today – so, so easy. She moved backwards into a beautiful Biellmann spin. Her right leg was perfectly vertical, stretching high above her head as she hooked the blade with her right hand and whirled around and around, staring upwards into the dazzling white light.

"Hey!"

Dreamily, Frankie realized that someone was speaking to her. She slowed and looked towards the barrier, trying to pick out Madame. Or was it the acid-tongued Valentine Dubois? She didn't recognize the voice.

"Hey!"

There it was again, louder now. Frankie peered into the darkness, jerking back in alarm as someone tapped her on the shoulder. She stumbled, her skates slipping from under her as she realized too late that she was going to—

"*Wake up!*"

With a start, Frankie opened her eyes as the bubble of her perfect dream popped.

"End of the line," said the bus driver, with an apologetic shrug. He returned to the front of the bus and slid open the doors so that Frankie, the only remaining passenger, could get off at the Olympic Village stop.

Blearily, Frankie descended the steps and shivered as the sub-zero blast of air hit her. Wrapping her scarf more securely around her neck and plunging hands deep into her pockets, she set off in the direction of the apartment, leaning forward into the icy wind. She thought longingly of a hot bath, heaped with bubbles, where she could forget about Valentine Dubois, Sophie LaFleur, Dylan... *everyone*.

"Frankie!"

Frankie sighed. Mentally, she waved goodbye to the relaxing bath because stalking towards her in knee-high boots, skinny jeans and a knee-length fake-fur coat was Madame von Berne. *Great*.

"What time do you call this?" snapped Madame, giving Frankie no opportunity to squeeze in an apology first.

Frankie pushed back her sleeve with clumsy mitten-clad fingers. "Erm…" She faltered, trying and failing to find her watch.

The coaching director tutted loudly. "It was a rhetorical question, Frankie," she said. "I know *exactly* what time it is. What I *don't* know is why you're late for a vitally important team dinner. Dylan rang. At least, I assume it was Dylan; there was an awful lot of noise in the background. So I worked out that you were all going to be late, which is why I'm not sitting like an idiot in the restaurant right now."

Haltingly, Frankie tried to explain, but excuses that had sounded so plausible in her head became weak and stupid as she voiced them. It was a rest day…they really wanted to see an Olympic event…

but the queues for the cable car were massive...
so they were stuck up the mountain...

Thankfully, she wasn't left to flounder for long.
Another bus pulled up at the stop and a crowd of
passengers emerged, among them Dylan, Paul,
Alesha and Scarlett. The four figure skaters hurtled
towards Madame and Frankie as if they were being
chased by an entire ice-hockey team. It soon became
clear that just after Frankie had left, the band had
quit playing for the day and there had been a rush
for the gondola.

"Glad you could all make it," said Madame von
Berne, in her driest voice.

"Why did you rush off?" whispered Alesha as
they waited nervously for Madame to explode. "I
looked for you in the crowd and couldn't find you.
Scarlett was stirring up trouble as usual – she told
me you were chasing some boy. As if you would,
eh?" She nudged Frankie. "So come on, then.
What's up?"

"Tell you later," Frankie said under her breath.
She caught sight of Dylan's thunderous expression
and her stomach clenched. Quickly, she stared

downwards to avoid his eyes, even though he was looking anywhere but her direction. "It's complicated," she said.

Alesha sighed. "You're not kidding. Dylan looks *really* mad. You look as if you've lost a gold medal and found a bronze. And Scarlett looks as if she's just won the Lipglosser of the Year award. She hasn't stopped smiling all evening."

"Everyone, *listen*!" snapped Madame.

There was an expectant silence.

But although the dressing-down was sharp, it was mercifully quick. Madame seemed to understand that the temptation of a real-life Olympic event was too hard to resist. However, she did remind them frostily that while they were away from home, they were in her charge. "So next time you have the urge to hike off to an altitude of 2000 metres, perhaps you'd like to tell me first…?" she finished.

Everyone nodded, hardly able to believe they'd got off so lightly.

"And now," said Madame, "let's eat."

* * *

The Italian restaurant was simply furnished, with wood-panelled walls, pine floorboards and red Formica tables. Edward, Anushka and the rest of Team GB were already tucking into sundried-tomato-topped bruschetta. Every other table was filled with chattering athletes and coaches.

"You took your time!" called one of the curling team, as Frankie and the others arrived. "Welcome to the Olympic Village's worst-kept secret! I have to warn you – the food's *fabulous*."

It was.

"Mmm…" sighed Alesha ten minutes later, as she cut another piece of four-cheese pizza.

"You won't be able to do a triple *anything* if you eat all of that," said Scarlett. She poked a fork into her salad and speared a cherry tomato, smiling snidely at Alesha before popping it in her mouth.

Alesha was unperturbed. "Just watch me," she said, readying her knife and fork for another attempt. "At least I won't be hungry when I've finished."

Frankie stifled a giggle, concentrating instead on tackling the heaped pasta dish in front of her.

She was sitting at the opposite end of the table from Dylan, separated from him by the entire curling team, who were loudly talking unfathomable tactics. So there was no danger of conversation between them. Frankie didn't know what she'd say anyway. And before she could ponder further, Madame *ting*ed her glass of sparkling water with a fork and the sporting babble around the table quietened. "I'll keep this brief," she began.

"Hurray!" cried one of the snowboarders. "Er… I mean…er…" He tailed off as Madame von Berne turned her withering gaze in his direction.

"I know that I speak for the other coaches when I say that you've all worked incredibly hard to be here," continued Madame as if no one had spoken. "I'd just like to remind you that you're representing your country. I want you to work hard, focus on the task in hand and try your *very* best." She paused and smiled round at them all, her expression softening for once. "I'm sure you're going to make me and everyone back home *very* proud."

"Yay!" cheered Scarlett, leaping to her feet and clapping. These weren't the polite, half-hearted and almost silent claps that the Ice Queen was usually known for, but great big, resounding ones.

Alesha rolled her eyes at Frankie and then shrugged apologetically. "If you can't beat them…" she said, getting to her feet too. Soon she was clapping as loudly as Scarlett.

Frankie hesitated only a moment before joining her. And within a few seconds, *everyone* was on their feet, cheering and whooping as if they'd already won Olympic golds, much to the bemusement of the Italian waiters, who shrugged at each other and joined in too. Madame Kristiana von Berne blushed wildly, but didn't tell them to stop. From beneath lowered lids, Frankie risked a glance towards the other end of the table, where Dylan was clapping as loudly as everyone else. But if he saw Frankie looking, he didn't let on.

All at once, Frankie felt her euphoria ebb away. Cheers echoing all around her, she sat down heavily and tried not to cry. Eventually, the noise died down and everyone returned to their seats.

"*Now* will you tell me what's wrong?" asked Alesha, her dark eyes anxiously searching for clues in Frankie's miserable face.

"There's been a bit of a mix-up with Dylan," whispered Frankie.

"So why don't you just talk to him about it?" asked Alesha. "Simple."

Frankie nodded as hope stirred within her. Alesha was right. She just had to tell Dylan that it had all been a silly misunderstanding. And in return, she would ask him to explain what was going on with Sophie LaFleur. She brightened at once, looking hopefully down the long table towards Dylan, hoping to catch his eye. But Madame von Berne chose that moment to lean forward, blocking Frankie's view.

"Now, if you've all finished," said the coach, looking pointedly at each of the seven figure skaters in turn, "I think it's time everyone got some sleep. Tomorrow is an important day. It's your final practice before the short program on Wednesday. Paul and Dylan, you go on ahead with the snowboarders. I'll settle the bill and then follow with the girls. I'd like to talk tactics." She smiled cheerfully, apparently unaware that she was scuppering Frankie's plans. "See you all bright and early tomorrow morning outside the apartment block."

Frankie watched unhappily as Dylan left the restaurant without a backward glance. She couldn't quite believe it. In the space of a single day, everything had changed. Her cherished dream of winning Dylan's heart had been dealt a serious blow. She longed for him to be her boyfriend. Now, it didn't even look like he was her *friend*. For all she knew, he and the gorgeous and talented Sophie LaFleur were already an item.

And in just a couple of days' time, Frankie was supposed to be competing in the biggest competition of them all...bigger than the British Junior Championships...bigger than Perfect Pairs... and bigger even than the prestigious World Figure Skating Championships. She was taking part in the *Winter Olympics*. After months of preparation, the world's biggest figure-skating event had arrived. Suddenly, Frankie knew why Madame had once told her to forget Dylan and focus on her skating... It was because boys got in the way. Because how was Frankie going to concentrate on the most important event of her life when she was worrying about Dylan?

And then there was Madame Valentine Dubois… What if she hadn't just been trying to knock Frankie's confidence? What if she was telling the truth? Had Frankie lost before the competition had even begun?

CHAPTER *Eight*

Frankie expected to be awake all night, but exhausted by the day's events, she slept soundly and dreamlessly. The next morning, she woke as the first rays of wintry sun shone through the gauzy bedroom curtains. And straight away she knew that she felt better. She swung her legs out of bed, grabbed her dressing gown and tiptoed to the door, careful not to disturb Alesha. A quick glance into the living room showed that it was empty. Phew. She didn't need Scarlett spoiling her good mood.

Frankie drew her dressing gown snugly around her and gazed at the city outside, where the sun was making everything sparkle. She felt a smile begin to tug at the corners of her mouth. Somehow, her worries had faded overnight. They hadn't gone…not exactly. She was still anxious to sort things out with Dylan. But on a fresh new morning like this it was impossible not to feel hopeful, and as she gazed at the glorious view, she gave herself a good talking-to about Madame Dubois until she was tingling with optimism about her Olympic dream once again. Frankie hadn't worked so hard and so long only to give up at the last minute. That would be unbelievably stupid. Instead, she was going to give it everything. She owed herself and she owed Madame von Berne that.

But first, she was going to have the lovely bubble bath that there hadn't been time for last night.

With a new spring in her step, Frankie hurried to the bathroom before Scarlett could beat her to it.

* * *

The minibus picked up the figure skaters at eight o'clock sharp, whisking them out of the Olympic Village, through the city streets towards a municipal ice rink on the outskirts. This was one of the practice rinks reserved for the competitors' use during the Olympics, because the official stadium itself was booked out with wall-to-wall events.

"Nervous?" whispered Alesha to Frankie as the minibus pulled up outside a modern red-brick building.

Frankie shook her head. "A little," she said truthfully. "But I'm looking forward to it too. I know it's only been a few days since we've skated, but I've missed it *so* much. I just want to get back on the ice now."

"Me too," said Paul, looking back over his shoulder at her.

Sitting next to Paul, Dylan stayed silent, staring ahead, then hurried down the steps as soon as the bus's doors slid open. Frankie hadn't even tried to speak with him this morning. It was obvious that he wasn't in the mood. She shrugged. If that was the way he wanted it, then fine. Frankie knew she had to focus on her figure skating. Swinging her bootbag over her shoulder, she followed Dylan and the others.

"Er…I'll see you rinkside," Madame von Berne called after them, her voice distracted.

Frankie was the last one to get off the bus and the only one who heard her. She looked back and saw that Madame was staring fixedly at her mobile phone, two spots of colour burning on her cheeks.

"I just got a text message… There's someone I need to meet…um…have a brief…er…" The coaching director's voice petered out. "Coffee," she finished, almost to herself. "Yes, that's what we'll have – a coffee." A series of emotions flitted across her face as Frankie watched. There was shock, definitely. And she was pretty sure there was happiness *and* sadness too.

"Bye," murmured Frankie, not even sure that Madame heard. It wasn't often that the coaching director's perfect composure crumbled, but it was crumbling now. And somehow, it felt wrong that Frankie was here to witness it happening.

Almost tripping in her haste to escape, Frankie hurried down the few steps and raced after Alesha, for the millionth time trying to work out what made Madame Kristiana von Berne tick. She was curt and snappy, often cross and sometimes downright *mean*. She was a brilliant coach, but a tough one too. She didn't have any time for weakness. She didn't encourage relationships between her skaters. She wasn't even keen on friendships, insisting that skaters should always be focused on their goal: to win. In fact, Madame frowned upon *anything* that distracted her protégées from figure skating. Meanwhile, her own private life was very mysterious. She'd told Frankie a little of her background at the Worlds, but all anyone else knew of her career was based on random gossip among the other skaters and the brief biography on the internet...

Madame Kristiana von Berne had once been a world-class figure skater. She had been competing at the 1982 World Figure Skating Championships in Copenhagen when the accident happened. Her short program had been awarded the highest scores ever. All she had to do was skate a moderately good long program and the gold medal would have been hers. But she seemed to lose concentration during her triple loop, caught an edge on landing... and it was over. She was stretchered off with an ankle broken so badly that she would never skate competitively again. The last view that millions of TV viewers had of the wonderfully talented figure skater Kristiana von Berne was of her sobbing into the camera that *"everything was ruined"*.

But although Kristiana von Berne's figure-skating career was finished, she returned a few seasons later in her new guise as a top coach. She was brilliant, inspiring and tough – *very* tough. She moved to the UK, where she soon hooked up with Team GB. Rumours were rife about why she'd left her home and switched allegiances to another country, but Madame simply told the press that she wanted "a new challenge". And no, she wasn't going to tell her story to the Sunday newspapers – or anyone else for that matter. So the only person who really knew the truth was Madame von Berne.

As Frankie laced up her beautiful white figure skates – custom-fitted, worn in but not worn out, and polished until they gleamed – she smiled wistfully. On the few occasions that the coaching director didn't terrify Frankie, she felt sorry for her. Outside figure skating, Madame Kristiana von Berne seemed to have *nothing*.

"When you've *quite* finished daydreaming…" said Alesha, standing with her hands on her hips. "I can guess who *you're* thinking about. Let me guess… Tall, red hair, tipped for gold—"

"Er, no…actually," Frankie cut in.

"Whatever," said Alesha, clearly not believing her. She pointed to the changing room exit. "There's a rink outside and I'd quite like to skate on it *before* the next ice age."

Giggles bubbled up inside Frankie and by the time she and Alesha had pushed through the heavy swing doors, she was spluttering with laughter. But as she stared at the expanse of ice before her, Frankie became silent. She was spellbound.

Olympic flags decorated the perimeter, but this place was nowhere near as dazzling as the Olympic stadium they'd visited the day before. This was just an everyday ice rink. It was in need of a coat of paint and the barrier encircling the rink was scarred with the collisions of a thousand beginners. It reminded her so much of the rink where she'd learned to skate. Like Lee Valley Ice Rink, this place was well-worn and well-loved. Today, it was reserved for the Olympic figure skaters and so far, there were only a few of them here. But usually, it would be teeming with a mixture of skaters – once-a-year skaters, those who spent more time on their bottoms than they did on their blades, those who were learning to jump, experts… All levels and all abilities would come here.

Frankie sighed dreamily. Places like *this* were what skating was really all about.

"Have aliens stolen your brain today, or what?" demanded Alesha. "In case you'd forgotten, it's the Olympic short program tomorrow. We've just got time to warm up and then we all run through our programs to the music. Let's skate!" She hopped through the gap in the barrier and glided quickly away, her movements charged with energy.

Suddenly, Frankie was fizzing with excitement. She stepped forwards, revelling in the magical feeling of metal on ice as she shuffled her blades to and fro. She glanced casually around the rink. Practice sessions were strictly regulated and Dylan and Paul were waiting for their turn on the ice, beyond the barrier. They were deep in conversation and she could see from here that Dylan was angry about something. Was he angry about *her*? Frankie sighed, and wished that Dylan would just talk to *her* about it. Sick of it all and determined to ignore him as much as he was ignoring her, Frankie set off towards the opposite end of the rink. She concentrated on making her movements smooth and regular, gliding left-right-left-right until she'd got used to the feel of the ice again. As she glided past the cafeteria area, Frankie caught sight of Madame von Berne out of the corner of her eye. She was with someone, a man. But he was huddled inside a jet-black ski jacket, his face hidden. All Frankie could see was his dark hair and greying temples. By the time she looked back, he was head-down, moving swiftly away. Madame remained behind, both hands clasped around a takeaway cup of coffee as if her life depended on it.

Frankie continued on her way, gliding forward on one foot and swaying to the left and to the right as she alternated edges. Then she did the same on the other foot. She carved an impromptu three-turn and moved backwards into a double toe-loop. "Ooh," she breathed as a feeling of pure exhilaration coursed through her. Now she was ready for something more adventurous. Not her entire short program, not yet. It wasn't her turn. First, she wanted to let herself go, and she knew the perfect move – a death drop.

The death drop was a daring mixture of camel spin in the air and sit spin on landing. Frankie loved it. Making sure there was no one in the vicinity, she surged forward on her left foot, knee well bent, arms and right foot extending behind her. Then, mustering all her strength, she pulled her arms forward and powerfully straightened her left leg. *Whoosh!* She leaped into the air. At the same time, she swung her right leg round until, for a moment or two, she seemed to hang in mid-air in a perfect spread-eagle position, staring down at the sparkling, gleaming ice. And then she returned to earth, landing softly on her right toe and bending down to absorb the impact, before leaning into a back sit spin with her left leg stretched in front of her. The rink and the skaters blurred as she spun round quickly. When she felt herself slowing, Frankie exited the move by rising into an upright spin.

The death drop wasn't in Frankie's routine, which meant that it was one of the few moves she hadn't practised a hundred times a day for the last few months. Which was perhaps why it felt *so* good. Frankie grinned to herself as she slowed.

"What do you think *you're* smiling about?"

Frankie jerked round, almost losing her footing. She recognized the voice – and the barely concealed nastiness in the other girl's tone – but it wasn't until she faced Sophie LaFleur that she saw the fury in the other girl's eyes. Staring right back, Frankie dug a toe pick in the ice to steady herself.

"Don't you think you should be practising something, well...a little more imaginative?" Sophie snarled. "You're not going to win gold with a death drop, you know."

Frankie felt as if she'd been punched. First Madame Dubois had given her a hard time and now Sophie LaFleur was doing the same... Did *no one* think she was any good? Frankie tried to stay calm. "It's not *in* my program," she said through gritted teeth.

"So what's *in* your program?" asked Sophie. "Bunny hops and spread eagles? They'd suit a beginner like you." She laughed and then swept away, performing three double Axels in quick succession.

Trembling with anger, Frankie watched her go. It took several deep breaths until she was calm again. She and Madame had been working on her Olympic short program for months. Frankie knew it so well, she could have skated it backwards. It was technically challenging, with enough required elements to keep the toughest judge happy, but it was quirky and entertaining too. And until now, Frankie had thought that it was pretty good... Suddenly, she wasn't so sure.

Too annoyed to go for anything more difficult, Frankie glided into a camel spin. She sailed

forwards, her free leg ramrod straight and stretched *so* high—
    Wham!

CHAPTER *Nine*

Frankie's legs flew from beneath her and she crashed to the ice, landing heavily on her side. She could have sobbed with frustration. She knew already what had happened: she'd been rammed by another skater – and it *so* wasn't an accident. Gingerly, she wriggled her fingers and toes to make sure nothing was broken. Thankfully, everything seemed to be working. But it was like Frankie's first day at the Ice Palace all over again. Then, it was Scarlett who had cannoned into her and sent her flying. And it didn't take Sherlock Holmes to work out who had done it this time.

"Ow!" she moaned, rubbing what she knew would soon be a massive bruise on her hip. "That *hurt*…"

"Are you okay?" gasped Alesha, crouching down beside her. "Is anything broken? I saw everything. It was—"

"Sophie LaFleur?" groaned Frankie.

Alesha nodded.

"Thought so." Frankie scanned the rink for the other skater. Already, Sophie had fled to the far end of the rink, where she was smiling prettily as she glided past Dylan, who had just walked up to the barrier. "I didn't see *that* coming," she muttered angrily.

"Come on," said Alesha, helping Frankie to her feet. "Don't let her put you off. Just forget all about her and run through your routine. I think it's your turn to skate to the music next. I'll watch out for her, okay?"

Frankie nodded glumly. Taking a deep, steadying breath, she started again. But all the excitement she'd felt earlier had evaporated, taking her confidence with it. Her movements were awkward and her transitions jerky, which meant that the different elements of her routine were oddly disconnected. She could have screamed. She was skating like a *beginner*, just like Sophie had said.

The routine was a total mess.

Frankie skidded to a halt, pressing the heels of her hands into her eyes in a vain attempt to stop the tears. This was crazy. Here she was, actually *at* the Winter Olympics, a day away from the short program, and she was all over the place. How was she going to bring it all together for the competition tomorrow?

"Frankie!" called Madame von Berne, beckoning Frankie from the ice. "We need to talk."

The good news was that Madame von Berne had seen everything. She'd seen Frankie felled by her rival. She'd seen – with relief – that with the exception of her pride, Frankie was uninjured. And she'd seen the effect the fall had on Frankie's skating. At once, she supplied her with a mug of steaming hot chocolate and made her sit down until she was calmer.

The bad news was that instead of sympathizing with Frankie, Madame brushed away the incident with a wave of her perfectly manicured fingers and instructed Frankie to "get over it".

"You are better than her," said Madame, whisking away the cardboard cup as soon as Frankie had finished her hot chocolate. Briskly, the coaching director pointed her back in the direction of the rink. "Now, go and prove it."

And to her surprise, Frankie did.

"It was the weirdest thing," she said to Alesha later that day. "If Madame von Berne had been sympathetic, I would probably have freaked out and then cried like a baby. Instead, she gave me no choice but to have another go." She shrugged helplessly. "And do you know what? It felt *great*. I think that might have been my best triple Salchow *ever*."

Alesha grinned. "It was stunning," she agreed.

A visit to the physiotherapist had confirmed that other than a purply-black bruise in the shape of

Cumbria on her leg, Frankie had not suffered any damage in the fall, so now she was doing her best to focus totally on tomorrow's big event.

She had decided not to think of Dylan and his beautiful green eyes, and she'd ignore Sophie and her catty remarks too.

Fabulous figure skating was what counted now.

It was as if someone had pressed fast-forward. The afternoon flew by in a flurry of exercise, practice, massage and pep talks from a totally hyped Madame. "Take your confidence, your dazzle, your boots and your outfit to the rink, but leave all distractions at the apartment," she told them. "And that includes mobile phones, Scarlett Jones." Scarlett tutted. Everyone knew that she was virtually welded to her iPhone. Afternoon melted into evening. Evening dissolved into bedtime and then into restless sleep.

At breakfast the next morning, Frankie managed to eat enough food to keep functioning, but didn't taste any of it. And then the morning was swallowed up by an official practice, followed by a long and very dull press conference, during which Madame von Berne told a roomful of reporters that she didn't expect a gold medal from her figure skaters. She was confident that Team GB would win at least two.

Frankie gulped. She *really* wanted to win one of those medals. She couldn't help glancing towards Dylan and their eyes met. At once, it was as if the stupid misunderstanding at the snowboard cross event had never happened. A cool shiver rushed through Frankie and her skin prickled with goosebumps. Even though he had been weirdly quiet since the snowboard cross, Dylan still made her feel as tingly as ever. But then she remembered his shameless flirting with Sophie and she quickly turned away. When she did look back, Dylan was staring hard at Madame, who was curtly telling a young reporter that there was no point asking whether she would step down as coaching director if her skaters didn't win, because they *were* going to win.

Next stop was the huge Olympic stadium, now

swamped with press and public. It was the women's figure skating short program this afternoon, but the entire team was going along to lend their support.

"Make sure you dazzle them!" called Paul, as the girls headed towards the changing room.

"I will!" sang Scarlett. "There are so many sequins on my outfit, the judges are going to need sunglasses to score me."

Alesha burst out laughing. "Nice one, Miss Jones," she said. "And there was me thinking that you didn't have a funny bone in your body."

Scarlett just stared at her. "Huh?" she said. "There are ten thousand hand-stitched sequins on my dress, Alesha Pattinson. I'm not joking – I'm going to be so dazzling they *will* need sunglasses." And she flounced into the changing room, oblivious to the stifled giggles in her wake.

Fresh from the news conference, Madame stalked after Scarlett. Frankie and Alesha followed them both, laughter soon forgotten and their thoughts already returned to the Herculean task ahead.

The air in the changing room was sticky with

hairspray, clouds of it billowing everywhere as figure skaters tried to make their hairstyles windproof. All around, there was chiffon and silk and tulle, from palest ivory to blackest black – and everything in between.

As they made their way over to the small area reserved for Team GB, Frankie gazed at the other girls' outfits. Wow… Up close, some of the dresses looked garish and over the top. The powernet holding them together looked clumsy and so obvious. But Frankie knew that once the wearers were out on the ice, the thick orangey-brown powernet would be invisible and the pantomime sparkle would fade until there was just the right amount of twinkle.

She was admiring the sky-blue catsuit of the Romanian skater when Frankie accidentally brushed against a jutting elbow.

"Ow!" screeched an outraged voice.

Frankie sighed heavily as the other girl whirled to face her, a messy stripe of eyeliner scrawled across her face. It was Sophie LaFleur, of course.

"You did that on *purpose*," snarled Sophie.

And all at once, Frankie lost it. She didn't care that she was supposed to concentrate on the biggest event of her life. She didn't care that Madame was probably listening and she'd be in big trouble later. She was fed up of the other girl walking all over her. "What, like you rammed me at the practice rink?" said Frankie.

"W-what?" The other girl was temporarily silenced, but it wasn't long before she recovered her poise. "I don't know what you mean," she said, blushing. "If I *did* brush against you at the rink – and I seriously doubt that – then it must have been an accident. I can win on my own merits, thank you. Tripping up the opposition is not my style."

All at once, Frankie felt her anger drain away. There was nothing to be gained from arguing just before a competition. "Let's just save this for the ice rink, shall we?" she said. "Do excuse me. I have a routine to skate." And she quickly walked away.

"Go, girl…" said Alesha, as Frankie joined them. "That told *her*."

Frankie blew out a plume of air. "I probably shouldn't have done that," she said, feeling a little worried now that adrenalin was no longer surging through her. She didn't feel quite so brave now.

Alesha regarded her seriously. "Yeah, probably not," she said. "But I'm glad you did!" And she flung her arms around Frankie in a celebratory hug.

"If you girls have quite finished," said Madame, "I believe we have a competition to win?" She raised an eyebrow as she looked at them.

Frankie had the distinct impression that Madame von Berne had overheard everything. Was she mad with Frankie for losing it…? But after a few seconds, the coaching director broke eye contact and Frankie breathed a sigh of relief. She was off the hook.

Madame von Berne delved into her expensive-looking handbag. "I wanted to show you all this before you skated," she said softly. Unfolding a sheet of paper, she smoothed it out and then held it up so that Scarlett, Alesha and Frankie could read the e-mailed message. The paper trembled very slightly in the coach's slender fingers.

It was from the British Olympic Association.

"*We know you can do it*," it said. "*Now, go for it, Team GB. Bring back medals.*"

"Right," said Madame, briskly folding up the message without comment. "You know how it goes. You're divided into groups of six. Each group warms up and then they skate in turn. The overall running order is as follows. Olga Krugalov the Russian skater is first. Then you're on, Scarlett. Sophie LaFleur is next. Then it's you, Alesha. And then there are a number of skaters before you, Frankie." She looked uncomfortable. "In fact, you're last."

"*Last?*" cried Frankie, her heart sinking. No one wanted to be last. The final skater had to hang around for so long, hardly able to watch the scoreboard, yet unable to look anywhere else. And meanwhile, figure skates scored and pitted the rink, each mark making the ice that little bit less smooth and that little bit more tricky for those who came after. "I suppose that at least I'll know what score I have to beat," Frankie said, with a wry smile.

"Correct," said Scarlett, smoothing her pink sequinned dress. "And that'll be *my* score, Frankie Wills," she said. "Because *I* am going to score *big*."

Frankie couldn't help laughing. "Go for it, Scarlett," she said. On impulse, she reached out for the other girl's hand and, ignoring her surprised expression, shook it firmly. "May the best girl win."

"Hear, hear!" said Alesha.

CHAPTER *Ten*

In the short program, Alesha beat her personal best with 63.02 points.

Scarlett did well, very well. She scored 68.76 points.

Olga Krugalov did even better, scoring 71.36 points.

And Sophie LaFleur, who dazzled the crowd with a brilliant interpretation of the Olympic theme music, beat them all with 76.50 points.

Frankie watched them all on the tiny TV at the

warm-up rink. And then, as her nerves increased, she returned to the changing room. In a vain attempt to fill the huge wait before her performance, Frankie listened to her iPod. But she couldn't concentrate on the music and eventually pulled out her earphones. She added another coat of lipgloss. She looked quizzically in the mirror. Should she go for more glitter? No, any more make-up and she'd look like a pantomime dame… Frankie sat in the slowly quietening changing room, listening to the instrumental music from the other performances that filtered through from the huge rink.

Blankly, she stared into the mirror. The girl staring back at her wore a striking dress of mauve and pink. Made of shiny satin, it had a fitted bodice that was dotted with glittering crystals. Long sleeves clung softly to her arms before flaring out at the cuffs. She turned slightly to admire the low back, which plunged downwards, held together with powernet. The short skirt had a ruffled hem that spun outwards when she whirled around. Urged on by Alesha, she'd applied silvery pink glitter to her eyelids and stuck on quite the biggest pair of false eyelashes ever. Her lipstick was soft pink. Frankie hardly recognized herself.

She looked like a princess.

"Ready?" asked a gentle voice.

Frankie looked away from the mirror and was shocked to see Madame there. And then she looked around and was even more amazed to see that there was only one other girl in the changing room. As Frankie watched, she left too. The changing room was empty of competitors, which could mean only one thing: it must be nearly her turn to warm up. Unsteadily, she got to her feet and stood swaying for a moment on her guards as she regained her balance.

She turned to look at Madame. "Now?" Frankie asked nervously. She could feel panic hovering like a bird of prey. Any minute now, it would pounce. "Only, I'm not sure I'm actually ready," she said. "I wonder if maybe I need a little more practice and if it would be more sensible if I saved myself for the next Olympics because—"

"Stop right there," said the coaching director, sounding calm, but firm. "You're more than ready," she said. "Now, come on. You have a short program to skate."

Frankie accompanied Madame to the warm-up area, where she clumsily removed the guards from her blades. Following the rules, she and the other five skaters limbered up on the ice for six short minutes. And then she went to wait for her turn to compete. She stared nervously at the sequinned blur beyond the barrier as the skater before her whisked to and fro, completing her routine. The other girl scored an unremarkable 43.84 points.

"Go on," said Madame, giving her a little push.

It was Frankie's turn. As she approached the barrier, she didn't think that she'd ever felt so truly terrified. She stepped into the rink, then paused, staring in growing horror at the expanse of ice before her, and beyond that the swathe of spectators. Every seat was filled. And every single spectator was watching her.

"*Skating for Great Britain, we have Frankie Wills!*" announced the commentator via the nasal-sounding PA system.

Frankie didn't move a millimetre. She felt frozen

to the spot. She couldn't skate in front of all those people and perform a medal-winning routine. She just couldn't.

"Hey," whispered a voice. "You *can*, Frankie. You *can* do it."

And then, with a rush of excitement, Frankie knew that whoever had spoken was right. She *could*. She moved one blade. Then the other. And then she was off, skating strongly and confidently towards the centre of the rink, where she slowed, pirouetted quickly and then stopped dead. Gracefully, she moved her arms around until one was aloft and one outstretched, like a ballerina on a musical box. She was ready.

Softly at first, the music began. Frankie pivoted on one toe before swooping around in ever increasing circles, seamlessly changing direction until she was powering towards her opening combination of triple Lutz and triple toe-loop. Both jumps were faultless and the audience's approval was deafening. On Frankie went, her blades flashing under the bright lights of the stadium as she twirled, flipped and twisted, dazzling the judges with the complex footwork that she'd worked so hard to perfect. Next, she flew into a triple flip, before swerving into a layback spin that transformed magically into her favourite move of all time, the Biellmann spin.

Frankie increased the speed and turned up the power. She was really going for it now. Her movements were quick and strong, her turns fluid, her arms graceful. Flying spin...step sequence... One by one, she ticked off the required elements. Her layback Ina Bauer received a special cheer as she glided forward on her left foot, her right foot angled out and her whole upper body leaning backward.

Frankie's final position was the same as her first – once again, she stood like the ballerina on the musical box. But now the spectators were on their feet too, applauding wildly. Bunches of flowers – each one wrapped in cellophane so that no petals would be left behind – sailed through the air, before landing to slide across the ice towards Frankie.

Shyly, she bowed to the audience and picked up the flowers before skating towards the gap in the barrier, where Madame von Berne was waiting with a smile. Frankie was unspeakably relieved. The short program was over.

"Excellent," said Madame. Her smile was both proud and wistful. "Very nearly perfect," she added.

Frankie couldn't believe her ears. Compliments from the draconian coaching director were virtually unheard of. But would the judges agree…?

Now came the really scary bit. Firmly, Madame escorted Frankie towards the kiss-and-cry area, where cameras from around the world were focused, ready to gauge the reactions of the skaters as they received their scores. Right then, Frankie knew what it really meant to be on the edge of her seat. Leaning forward, she tried and failed to decipher the stream of numbers read out.

In desperation, she looked questioningly at Madame.

"You scored 76.05 points," said the coaching director, her glossy red lips curving into yet another smile. "You're in second place, just 0.45 points behind Sophie LaFleur. Well done!"

"Frankie!" screeched a voice from the competitors' zone. "You're in the *silver-medal* position." It was Alesha, wild-eyed with excitement. "You rock!"

Blearily, Frankie remembered that, with a score of 63.02 points, Alesha was currently sixth, so she was almost certainly out of the running for a medal. But even so, it hadn't stopped her congratulating Frankie. Which all added up to the indisputable fact that Alesha was a true friend. Wordlessly, Frankie rushed over to her and hugged her tightly across the barrier.

"Hey, look who's talking to the reporters," said Scarlett, pointedly ignoring the fabulous score *and* the fact Frankie was doing better than the Ice Queen herself. Scarlett brushed past Frankie as if she weren't even there. "Sophie La-flipping-Fleur," she spat. "When is it *my* turn?"

Alesha rolled her eyes. But Scarlett's attention was very firmly focused on the small TV screen on the back of the camera.

"You did really great, Sophie," the Canadian reporter was saying. "We're all so proud of you. What do you have to say to your fans?"

"Oh, thank you *so* much," gushed Sophie, flicking back her blonde ringlets. "It means a lot to me that I have so much support." A sudden smile lit up her sharp face for a couple of seconds before vanishing just as quickly. She glanced down, fluttering her eyelashes prettily. And when she looked up, the gathered crowds sighed. Because Sophie LaFleur's green eyes were awash with tears. "It hurts me to say this..." she began.

The reporter leaned forward. "What is it, Sophie?" she asked gently. "You're in the gold-medal position at the Winter Olympics. What could possibly be wrong?"

Sophie sniffed a little, before turning her gaze towards the camera lens... Frankie was watching the tiny screen on the back of the film camera and it looked as if the other girl was staring straight at her with eyes as cold and as hard as steel.

"I have an enemy," Sophie said clearly. "*Someone* doesn't want me to do well in the Olympics. I-I-I've just discovered that..." She paused, as if it was almost too distressing for her to speak. And then she drew a shaky breath before continuing. "While

I was skating, *someone* stole my lucky mascot from the locker room. Someone knows how much Barney the bear means to me. I implore that *someone* to give him back." A member of the camera crew handed her a packet of tissues, and she daintily extracted one, dabbing her eyes.

"Oh, pur-lease," said Alesha. "This is the Olympics, not the Oscars. Who does she think she's kidding with the melodramatic speech?"

Frankie shrugged. "It's only a bear," she whispered back.

"It would be wrong of me to accuse anyone," Sophie went on, after regaining her poise, apparently with some difficulty. "I don't know if it's a fan who just wants a piece of me or maybe a jealous newcomer who thinks that they can beat me in the free skate and steal my gold medal…" She paused meaningfully, sniffed and then stared past the camera directly at Frankie.

"Oh no…" murmured Frankie, as she realized with horror that Sophie was talking about *her*.

Sophie looked back at the camera. "I just hope that *whoever* has stolen Barney will have the decency to return him. Because if I don't have him, th-th-then…" She blew her nose loudly. "If I *don't* find him before the free program…then I'm n-n-not even sure that I can compete." Her voice rising hysterically now, she added, "Without him, how can I *win*?" Sophie burst into tears, brushing aside the reporter's kind questions as she ran from the rink.

There was a brief, stunned silence before the reporter hurriedly told viewers that they were switching to the exciting action at the skeleton bobsleigh event.

Was it Frankie's imagination, or did people around her suddenly turn coldly in *her* direction…? After all, *she* was the newcomer around here. Had they seen who Sophie had been staring at? *Had they worked out that Sophie was blaming Frankie for the theft?*

Chapter *Eleven*

What started as a few hard stares after Sophie's impassioned speech quickly grew into something much, much bigger and a whole lot nastier. As soon as the tear-soaked TV interview ended, the rumours began.

The internet was awash with speculation.

Whodunnit? blogged one Canadian skating enthusiast. *Was it one of Sophie's rivals? An old enemy? A jealous newcomer? Someone who has a lot to gain if Sophie drops out?*

Then the finger-pointing got worse. The hints became stronger. And it became horribly clear that Frankie was the number-one suspect.

I wouldn't like to accuse anyone, was the message posted by another skating fan. *But let's call our thief F, for example… If this F were someone who is well known for her rebellious behaviour, then she might be the sort of person who would deliberately sabotage poor Sophie's chances. Right?*

"Wrong!" Alesha shouted at the computer screen when she read the latest comments. "I can't believe they're saying such things about you, Frankie. It's so unbelievably unfair. It's slander, that's what it is!"

Frankie shrugged. "They're not actually accusing *me*," she murmured. "This could be some other F they're talking about, I suppose…"

"Yeah, right," huffed Alesha, brushing messy black hair out of her eyes as she scanned the screen for more comments.

Fully aware that nothing she could say would make Alesha calm down, Frankie concentrated on the milky froth of her cappuccino as she slowly sipped her drink. They were hiding out in a quiet corner of the Olympic Village internet cafe. Since Sophie had revealed the theft of her prized mascot the day before, wherever Frankie went, she sensed that everyone was sneaking suspicious looks in her direction. But whenever she stared directly at them, they turned away. No one said anything to her face – and they didn't need to. Frankie knew what they were thinking. The really upsetting thing was that everyone seemed to have forgotten her near-perfect routine and fabulous score. In the space of one stupid TV interview, she'd gone from hero to zero.

Meanwhile, Scarlett Jones was behaving as if Christmas had come early. To Frankie's face she was saccharine sweet; behind her back, she was the biggest gossip of them all.

Even Dylan seemed to be avoiding Frankie. She didn't know if it was because of the misunderstanding with Breck or the Sophie situation. Or both. Whatever, he'd stayed well away from her after the short program.

But the worst thing of all was that the whole stupid situation was affecting Frankie's self-esteem.

She hated the feeling that everyone was thinking badly of her. And how could she skate when her confidence was at an all-time low?

One person who'd been surprisingly comforting was Paul. He had taken Frankie to one side and told her to ignore malicious gossip. "I can't believe there's so much fuss about a stupid soft toy," he said, shaking his head. "Keep a dignified silence and they'll soon get bored and move on to the next thing." Frankie wasn't so sure. The rumours showed no signs of abating. If anything, they were getting worse.

As Frankie drained her cup, a familiar voice dragged her away from her melancholy thoughts and back to the present.

"I wondered where you were hiding!"

Alesha rolled her eyes. "Oh, great," she said under her breath. "The Queen of the Ice has found us."

"Hi, Scarlett. Been shopping again?" Frankie said, readying herself for the inevitable onslaught. She didn't have long to wait.

"Oh, don't be such a misery guts," said Scarlett. She strolled towards them, monogrammed shopping bags swinging from both hands. "Anyone would think you'd just blown your chances at the Olympics." Then she threw up both hands as if the most delightful thought in the world had just occurred to her. "But I suppose that's exactly what you *have* done, isn't it?" she said gleefully. "You thought you were going to snatch the gold off Sophie LaFleur after the free skate and when the authorities launch an inquiry, they'll discover that you stole the local girl's lucky mascot. You're going to end up with *nothing*. Oh, Frankie…what a *silly* thing to do. You'll be disqualified when the judges find out who did it!"

This was nothing short of mean. Frankie opened and closed her mouth like a goldfish. For once, she was totally speechless. Ever since she'd met Scarlett, the other girl had thrown every weapon at her disposal at Frankie. Ever since she'd deliberately cannoned into her at the rink on Frankie's very first day at the Ice Palace, Scarlett had never missed the chance to hurt her with barbs and jibes. The mascot incident was her best opportunity yet.

Alesha stared fixedly at the screen. "The door's

that way, Scarlett," she said mildly. "I suggest you use it before I grab hold of your feet and do the headbanger move with you."

Despite her low spirits, Frankie found it hard not to laugh. The headbanger was a pairs move that involved spinning a female skater round by her feet in huge circles, while her head whizzed within millimetres of the floor. It was totally forbidden in international figure-skating competitions. It was also horribly dangerous.

"If you're really unlucky," added Alesha. "I'll let go."

Scarlett flinched. "There's no need to be nasty," she said.

"Why not?" said Alesha. "You are."

"Hmph," said Scarlett, flinging back a curtain of blonde hair. She turned back to Frankie. "*You* deserve everything you get. Look at you, waltzing in and stealing a valuable Olympics place from someone who's been learning the sport for years… It's logical that you'd try to steal a gold medal too. And if anyone asks me, I shall tell them just that." She spun on her heel and marched out of the room.

"Oh, Alesha…" said Frankie as the door swung shut. "You're fab! But maybe you shouldn't have said that…"

"Sorry," said Alesha. "She just gets me riled. And you're too nice to answer her back, so I'm doing it for you." She swung round in her seat and faced Frankie, her dark eyes serious. "Anyway, Scarlett is the least of your problems. You've skated one of the best routines of your life – your double Axel and triple Lutz combination was the best I've seen – yet Sophie LaFleur has still managed to steer everyone's attention away from the ice rink by telling lies. Her mascot hasn't been stolen. She's making it all up. But I don't get it. Why does she need to resort to underhand tactics to discredit you? She's a brilliant skater. If she wants to beat you, why doesn't she do it fair and square – on the ice rink?"

"You're jumping to conclusions," said Frankie. "If we accuse *her* of lying about the theft then that's just as bad as what she's doing to *me*."

"Pfft," said Alesha. There was no arguing with her. She was convinced of her theory and that was that.

Frankie wasn't so sure, but what she did know was that it didn't matter how long they debated the finer points of the Bear Hunt – as it had been nicknamed by the press. Unless the culprit or the missing bear were found, then Frankie remained under a cloud of suspicion, which wasn't a very pleasant place to be.

Luckily, the text that Frankie received just as they were about to leave the cafe saved her from being the most despondent competitor in the whole of the Winter Olympics. The wonderful – and very long – text was from Mum...

Hi Frankie! Guess who's coming to Canada to see you sk8?! Meeeeeeeee! (Don't ask how we got the £££ together – we just did, right?) Couldn't make it for the short program, but I'll be there for the free skate. I can't miss out on seeing my favourite eldest daughter win an Olympic medal, can I? Big hugs. Mum xxx

Frankie was *thrilled*, but she was nervous too. She hadn't told anyone back home about the nasty rumours. What would Mum say when she found out about the scandal? She'd be *so* upset.

And that would break Frankie's heart.

The situation worsened again the following morning when the local paper ran a story about the mysterious disappearance of Sophie LaFleur's lucky mascot. Frankie saw the headline as soon as she left the apartment on her way to the rink. *Will Olympic skaters stop at nothing to win gold?* she read through the window of the newspaper dispenser. Her stomach churned. Unable to resist, she fed the correct change into the slot and plucked out a copy.

It was toxic stuff.

Down at the Olympic ice rink, everyone's in a spin, said the article. *Rumours are rife that a newcomer has stolen the beloved mascot of local figure-skating star, our delightful Sophie LaFleur.*

While Sophie was skating her way to the top of the ladies' scoreboard with a sparkling routine, Barney the bear vanished in mysterious circumstances from the ladies' changing rooms. He hasn't been seen since and Sophie is devastated. It's been suggested that unless Barney is returned before the free program, the Canadian star will not compete.

"She's easily the best figure skater here," says her coach, the legendary Valentine Dubois. "To Sophie, Barney is more valuable than gold. He's all the luck she needs to win. And I hope that whoever has stolen him, returns Barney to his rightful owner. The thief should be punished. This is not a lot of fuss over a soft toy. This is a serious offence."

Frankie stuffed the newspaper in the nearest bin and walked quickly to the bus stop, blinking back the tears. Anyone who read that article would be in no doubt that it was talking about her. She was the newcomer.

But the article had got two things *very* wrong…

One. Frankie *hadn't* done it. Of course she hadn't. And what's more, she hadn't seen anyone else steal anything. So *who was* the thief?

Two. This *was* a lot of fuss over a soft toy. Frankie was sorry that Sophie's mascot was gone, but she didn't see how it should stop her competing. That sort of logic was silly. But Frankie was horribly afraid that it was the sort of silliness that would get her thrown out of the world's biggest and best figure-skating event.

Which brought her back to her first point: Frankie *hadn't* done it.

"Arghhh," she muttered.

The bus arrived, already half full of figure skaters who were bound for the practice rink, just like Frankie. She hurried to the first empty seat, keeping her head well down. *Why* hadn't she caught the earlier bus with Alesha? On her own, the hostility seemed so much worse. They were all staring at her. She knew they were. And as she felt accusing eyes bore into her back, Frankie began to doubt whether she could do this. Could she carry on taking part in a competition when there was so much bad feeling towards her?

If success was going to bring so much unhappiness…was it worth it?

Frankie just didn't know any more.

CHAPTER *Twelve*

By the time she reached the practice rink, Frankie's spirits were at an all-time low. She thought back to the time she'd gone skiing with the others, stupidly pretending that she knew what she was doing. Egged on by Scarlett, she'd fallen badly, twisting her knee and putting herself out of the European Juniors.

That had been bad...but this was worse.

Glumly, Frankie laced up her boots and took to the rink, trying to ignore the negative vibes that she was sure were coming from the other skaters and coaches. She stroked across the ice, reversing with a simple three-turn so that she was heading backwards. And then, keen to show all of them – not least herself – that she didn't care what they thought, she built up speed and went for the triple Salchow.

But as her toe pick left the ice and she sprang into the air, Frankie realized that she didn't have anywhere near enough power to spin three times. She barely managed one and a half rotations before landing awkwardly on her toe pick. And instead of gliding backwards strongly, she stumbled and fell forward onto her knees.

"Ow…" she said, sitting back on the ice and rocking to and fro. That had hurt.

"Serves you right," muttered another skater as they shot past. "Now you know how Sophie feels."

Frankie could hold back the tears no longer. Struggling to her feet, her blades slithering and slipping on the ice, she began to sob with frustration and with anger too. It was all just *so* unfair. Everyone was blaming her for something she hadn't done.

And now the worst of all possible things had happened...

The magic had gone from her skating.

She skidded towards the barrier, as ungainly as a duck on a frozen pond, the tears flowing down her cheeks. She'd officially had enough. There was no need for her even to go to the Olympic stadium tomorrow. She would retire from the competition and catch an early flight home. And then she'd go back to her old school and her old life in London.

Goodbye early starts and endless criticism at the rink.

Goodbye Ice Palace.

Goodbye figure skating.

At the barrier Frankie stopped dead as she remembered. Mum was flying thousands of kilometres to watch her compete... She clenched her eyes shut and realized that it didn't even matter about Mum coming over – Frankie wanted *out* and she wanted out *now*.

The first things Frankie saw when she stumbled blindly from the rink were the sleek leather boots. She sniffed and dragged her sleeve across her face to wipe away the tears. It was probably a journalist or a reporter. And she *really* didn't want to talk to them, not when they were the ones who were making the whole situation so much worse by printing lies about her.

"Excuse me," muttered Frankie, trying to push past the woman. She didn't budge and Frankie looked up. "Oh," she said.

"Come with me," said Madame Kristiana von Berne.

Frankie's resolve wavered. This was the woman who'd plucked her from obscurity and spent two and a half long, difficult years training her for the Olympics. Did Frankie have the nerve to tell her that she wanted out, right now? On the other hand…she'd made her mind up. So…

"M-Madame," Frankie began, "I need to talk to you."

"For goodness' sake," replied the coach. "This is neither the time nor the place to be having a discussion about *anything*. If you'll stop snivelling and come with me, we'll find somewhere more appropriate to talk."

Although Madame's voice was firm, it was not unkind and Frankie felt herself relaxing just a little. She pulled an old tissue from her tracksuit pocket and blew her nose noisily. This was probably for the best. At least she didn't have to go looking for the coaching director to quit. Madame had saved her the bother.

After retrieving Frankie's outdoor shoes from her locker and instructing her to change into them, Madame quickly hurried Frankie out of the building and onto a bus back to the Olympic Village. When they arrived, the coaching director took Frankie towards a cafe just beyond the athletes' quarters in a residential part of the city. Tucked away down a side street, the coffee shop they found was old-fashioned and oddly shaped, with threadbare velvet sofas and armchairs tucked into alcoves and around corners. Frankie chose a sofa on the far side. It was purple velvet, piled high with brightly coloured cushions and as she sat down, Frankie instantly felt more relaxed. She closed her eyes and sank back into the cushions. Mmm... It felt as if the sofa were hugging her. She wasn't even aware that Madame had gone to get drinks until a gentle clinking announced her return. Frankie opened her eyes reluctantly to see the coaching director carrying a fully loaded tray.

"Wow!" breathed Frankie, eyeing up the pile of chocolate muffins. "They look *amazing*."

Wordlessly, Madame passed a muffin and a mug of hot chocolate to Frankie. Then she rested the tray on a low table before picking up a tiny cup of coffee. The coach sipped her espresso, while Frankie bit into the muffin. It was melt-in-the-mouth delicious.

For a moment or two, there was a contented silence. And then Frankie swallowed the last mouthful and steeled herself for the words she knew would be so difficult to say. She tried to sit up a little in the wonderfully comfortable sofa and took a deep breath. "Madame—"

"No, you're not," said Madame quickly.

"But you don't know what I'm going to say!" Frankie protested.

"Yes, I do," the coach replied. "And no, you're not quitting."

"Oh," said Frankie. She felt curiously deflated.

"And what's more, I owe you an apology," Madame went on.

Now Frankie was confused too. "Pardon?"

The coaching director placed her cup on the table and, folding her arms, leaned forward a little. "I watched the TV interview with Sophie LaFleur, just like everyone else did," she said. "But I'm afraid that I didn't take it seriously. Sophie's accusation was quite obviously targeted at you, but it was so absurd that I truly believed that everything would blow over by the end of the day. I thought that you were well equipped to deal with the odd snide comment. And I thought that it was better if I didn't meddle—I can be heavy-handed sometimes..." She paused and gave a short, humourless laugh. "I've just read the headlines in today's papers. Quite clearly, I was mistaken. This silly business has gone too far."

There was no hope of Frankie finding her voice now. As far as she knew, Madame von Berne had never admitted to being wrong, ever. Which made this entirely uncharted territory.

"I'm so sorry, Frankie," Madame went on. "I've just spoken with Alesha, who tells me how bad it's been for you. And I've seen for myself how it's affected your skating, which makes this a *very* serious situation. It's logical that you're thinking of leaving us…and the Olympics."

Frankie gave a small nod.

"Now, how about you tell me what's happened since you arrived at the Olympic Village," said Madame softly. "I want to know *everything*. And let's see if we can get to the bottom of this mess. Because the last thing I want is for my star performer to rush back home when there's a place on top of the Olympic podium with her name on it."

Star performer? Frankie opened her eyes as wide as they would go. Was that what Madame thought of her? And did she really believe that Frankie could win gold? Suddenly, hopping on a plane back to the UK didn't seem quite such a sensible idea. And if she stayed, Mum might never know that there'd been a problem…

"First," said Madame, "let me get another coffee." She went to the counter. "An espresso, please,"

Frankie heard her say. "And make it a double shot. I think I'm going to need it." She returned to her seat. "Start at the beginning, please."

So Frankie did. She told Madame about the trip to the snowboard cross, how she'd come back earlier than the others and how she'd shared a gondola with Valentine Dubois. At this, Madame's carefully plucked eyebrows shot up, though she said nothing. Frankie mentioned the incident at the rink, where Sophie had crashed into her. And finally she went over the events at the short program. "But I didn't steal Sophie's mascot!" she finished. "Why would I do such a thing?"

The coaching director rolled her eyes. "Of *course* you didn't do it," she said.

"Madame?" ventured Frankie. A thought had been nagging at her for a while now and she had to say it. "I'm starting to think that sporting events aren't very…well…*sporting*," she finished. "I hadn't realized how totally ruthless some people can be."

At first, the coaching director didn't speak. She examined her fingernails for so long that Frankie thought she'd forgotten about her. Eventually, she spoke. "Did you know that Valentine Dubois and I were once rivals?" she said.

This was news.

"We competed in the Junior Worlds and she won silver to my gold," Madame said quietly. "She wasn't happy about it, as you can imagine. So, when we both took part in the Worlds a couple of years later, she was determined to win. So was I. As you know, I fell." She pressed her glossy lips together for a few seconds until they stopped trembling.

Frankie chewed her lip, afraid to break the silence.

Then Madame recovered her poise and gave a humourless smile. "Unfortunately for Valentine," she went on, "she didn't win either. She missed out on the bronze by a whisker. But…" The coaching director stopped.

"But…?" prompted Frankie.

"But *nothing*," snapped Madame, abruptly back to her brisk, businesslike self. She looked right at Frankie. "Put everything that Valentine Dubois said out of your mind – clearly, the woman wants to get back at me, by sabotaging *your* Olympic dreams. Forget about Sophie LaFleur too – I strongly suspect that it's Valentine who has egged her on – and I'll do my best to quell the nasty rumours. But most importantly, what you must do is *believe* in yourself again." By now, her cheeks were flushed and her tone urgent. "Of all the skaters I have ever met in my long career, Frankie," said the coach, "you have the most flair, the most passion and the most brilliant technical ability. You are the most naturally talented. I couldn't have trained anyone else to Olympic standard in such a short time. *Don't* waste that talent. Please."

"Oh," said Frankie, vaguely aware that she was spending a lot of this morning being totally gobsmacked. Now was no exception.

"Other skaters fear you because they know you're good," said Madame. "Deep down, Sophie LaFleur knows that she can't beat you. You're innocent and you must do your best to rise above these stupid accusations."

Frankie nodded. This was an awful lot to take in, but she *knew* that Madame von Berne was right about ignoring the bad press. And as for the huge compliment about her talent… Well, that was almost too much to take in. "Madame?" she said.

"Yes?" said the coaching director, getting to her feet and buttoning her leather jacket.

"I don't think I'm going to quit after all," said Frankie sheepishly.

"I know," said Madame. "You never were." She deposited a couple of notes on the table before flinging her handbag over her shoulder. "See you later, Frankie," she said. "Why don't you go back to the apartment and get some rest?"

Frankie watched her go, unsure whether to feel offended, relieved or just plain surprised. She began to smile…and then giggle…and soon she was laughing so hard that she thought she might cry again. Finally, worn out by the emotions that had been flooding through her today, she reached for another muffin. If she had a gold medal to win, then she was going to need it.

CHAPTER *Thirteen*

After she left the coffee shop, Frankie caught the first bus back to the Olympic Village. There was something very important she needed to do.

She needed to talk to Dylan.

They hadn't spoken since the snowboard cross event and she needed to know where they stood. If he wanted to go out with Sophie, then of course she'd be upset. But she *would* get over it. If, on the other hand, Dylan's silence was just because of the silly misunderstanding with Breck, then they should sort things out as quickly as possible.

After all, she didn't want to lose one of her best friends.

As soon as she reached the Olympic Village, Frankie checked out all of the usual places, looking for him. But Dylan wasn't in the boys' apartment, the internet cafe or the pool hall. He must be at the practice rink – and she definitely wasn't going back there. Frankie sighed, frustrated that her big speech would have to wait.

Deep in thought, she walked back to the Olympic Village's internet cafe. And, hiding herself away in the corner, she quickly logged on. There were stacks of messages waiting for her: from her dad; from her brother Josh and from Rosie, her oldest friend. All of them wanted to know about Sophie and the missing mascot. She sighed, gutted that the news had reached as far as the UK. Deciding that she'd reply to them later, she surfed the internet, clicking on the link to a figure-skating news site. Perhaps she'd find something *there* that didn't involve her or a cuddly toy.

Her eyes widened at the latest entry.

International figure-skating heavyweight Madame Kristiana von Berne has now waded into the bitter row about Sophie LaFleur's missing bear, the blogger had written. *In an interview with a major TV network, the Team GB coaching director said that the thinly veiled accusations against Frankie Wills were ill-founded and nothing short of libellous. "I would be grateful if everyone would stop harping on about this ridiculous non-event and turn their attention to what we are* meant *to be talking about. And that's the greatest sporting event on earth. The Olympics."*

Below the article, readers had already posted a range of replies. Unbelievably, most of them supported Madame.

Frankie found that she was smiling. *Wow.* Madame had been true to her word. And just like that, the tide had begun to turn. Grabbing the mouse, Frankie whizzed to another website, where she found the same story. She leaned back in her chair and clasped both hands behind her head, wondering if Madame's comments would make a difference to the way she was being treated here in the Olympic Village. So much had gone wrong that she hardly dared hope.

Her eyes flitted around the internet cafe, alighting on the wall clock. There was an eight-hour time difference between here and home, but there was a slim chance that someone would be up by now. She'd call them to take her mind off things.

She clicked on the icon for video conferencing and dialled up the Wills' household, waiting anxiously while it rang and rang.

"*Nnng?*" groaned a voice as the other webcam activated, showing a pyjama-clad Josh. He stared blearily at the screen. "Do you know what time this is? Some of us have school tomorrow…er, today." He rubbed his eyes and shouted, "Dad! It's that annoying Olympic athlete that keeps bugging us. Do you want to talk to her while I go back to bed?" There was a faint mumbling noise in the background.

"Cheers," said Frankie, grinning. She and her big brother didn't say a polite word to each other if they could help it. But it didn't mean that they didn't get on. "Go on, then," she added, peering closely at the screen. "You *definitely* need your beauty sleep."

"Ha," said Josh. He winked and vanished.

Mum came into view. "Darling!" she cried. "How *are* you? I'm leaving for the airport in a few minutes! I can't believe that I'm going to see you tomorrow!"

Frankie grinned. She could hardly believe it either.

Before Frankie could reply, Dad appeared too. "Hey!" he croaked. "How's the triple flipping?"

"Bob!" said Mum quickly. "It's a triple *flip*." She glared at Frankie's dad and poked him in the ribs. "*Stop it*."

Frankie giggled. "So what did you think of the short program?" she asked.

They'd watched it on television and Mum was full of praise for her "bellboy spin".

"And her triple loots," added Dad. "Don't forget those!"

"Biellmann spin and triple Lutz…?" asked Frankie, trying not to smile.

"Er…that's what we said," replied Dad, scratching his head and appearing genuinely confused.

For a few wonderful minutes, it was just like being at home. Frankie filled her parents in on what she'd been up to, skimming over the details about Sophie's mascot. In return, they told her the new words that her young twin sisters had learned this week – *Olympics*, *gold* and *medal* – and how everyone they knew was rooting for her.

"I can't wait to see you on that podium, sweetheart," said Dad softly. "Even if it is just on the telly."

"And I can't wait to see you on the podium *in true life*!" cried Mum. Then she frowned. "Just mind your step when you climb up there. You don't want to trip up like Robin Cousins when he won gold in 1980. He nearly went head over skates."

"I'll be careful," Frankie said, "*if* I get there." She checked the time. "Look, I've got to go. See you tomorrow, Mum. I wish you were here, Dad."

"I'll be watching it live," Dad promised.

Mum just grinned.

They said their goodbyes and Frankie rubbed at her eyes quickly. But she was determined not to cry again. She'd done enough of that for one Olympics. Instead, she returned to the apartment and plugged in her iPod. Exhausted by the morning's events, she was asleep before the end of the second track.

"Hey, wake up!"

It was Alesha's voice, but it was coming from far away and Frankie wanted so desperately to ignore it. But she couldn't ignore the shaking and prodding and reluctantly she opened her eyes to see that the room was dark. She sat bolt upright. Had she slept all afternoon *and* all night? *Was it time for the free program already?*

"It's dinner time!" said Alesha, clicking on the bedside light. "I didn't think you'd want to miss that. We're eating in the athletes' canteen in the village tonight." She peered down at Frankie when there was no response. "You are coming, right?"

"Er…yeah," said Frankie. Sleepy and disorientated, she knew that there was something she needed to do… In a flash, she remembered. "Course I am," she told Alesha. "Just give me a minute to get ready?"

They walked into the crowded canteen together just ten minutes later. It was buzzing with noise and chatter. Was she imagining it, or was Frankie getting fewer hard stares than earlier? Was she officially off the hook?

One of the speed skaters threw a weird look in Frankie's direction and her heart sank. Not *everyone* believed Madame's statement then…

"Hey!"

Frankie watched as Breck sauntered towards them wearing baggy jeans, a hoody and a lazy grin. He looked delighted to see her.

"Oh, good," muttered Alesha, who had decided that she didn't approve of Breck's heavy-handed flirting. "It's Mr. Smooth come to cause more trouble."

"Hey, Breck," said Frankie guardedly. She stuffed her hands into her pockets so that the snowboard champion couldn't hold them, but he simply looped an arm around her shoulders instead.

"How's it going?" he asked, pointedly ignoring Alesha, who was glaring at him.

"Oh, you know, the usual sort of stuff," replied Frankie. "Trying to quash rumours that I'm a pickpocket, practising for an Olympic routine..." She tried to shrug off Breck's arm and failed miserably. "Anyway, what do you want? I wouldn't have thought you'd want to hang around with me after Sophie virtually branded me a thief."

"Oh, I don't worry about things like that," Breck drawled, totally missing the sarcasm in her voice. "It makes you more *exciting*. What was it you stole anyway? Her cat?"

"Er, hello...?" said Frankie. "There's no way I'd ever steal anything. For the record," she added, "it was Sophie's cuddly bear that went missing. If you find it, please do return it to her. Because I haven't got it." At last, she managed to shake him off and turned her back, helping herself to a tray. She had better things to think about, like dinner.

"Hey, whatever," said Breck. He took a tray and joined the queue behind Frankie, apparently oblivious to the frosty looks that Alesha was sending in his direction. "So," he said, pushing along his tray with one hand and draping the other over her shoulder again. "All ready for tomorrow's big event?"

Frankie grimaced at Alesha. "How do I get rid of him?" she mouthed at her friend.

Alesha shrugged helplessly.

But as Frankie was trying to come up with a brilliant plan to gag Breck – who was now listing his race times and telling her that he'd start teaching her how to snowboard as soon as she'd won gold – she saw Dylan.

With the world's worst timing, he appeared in the doorway of the canteen, scanned the room and spotted Frankie almost immediately. For a millisecond, they stared at each other and then Breck reclaimed her attention by asking her if she was "goofy" or "non-goofy", whatever that meant. When she looked back, Dylan was striding purposefully through the canteen, and out of the corner of her eye she saw Sophie LaFleur waving madly at him. Her heart sank. Frankie knew exactly what was about to happen. Dylan would blank

Frankie like he had at the snowboard cross party and sit with her arch-rival instead.

But he *didn't*.

Dylan walked right up to *Frankie*.

"Hi," he said softly, self-consciously pushing his floppy chestnut hair away from his eyes as he spoke.

"Hi!" she said, swivelling round so that Breck's arm slipped off her shoulders. She smiled uncertainly. He didn't *look* angry, which was a start.

"Can we have a chat?" asked Dylan.

"Dude!" said Breck, suddenly realizing that they had company. "Dylan, isn't it? I was just telling Frankie about the snowpark. I'm going to show Frankie a couple of moves on the half-pipe once she's won that medal. She's going to *love* it." He replaced his arm on Frankie's shoulder. Yet again, she shook it off. "Hey, what's up?" he asked her.

"I'd...um...like to talk to Dylan," Frankie said.

"Yeah, but you're with me right now," replied Breck, looking confused.

"No, *dude*," said Dylan. "She's with *me*."

CHAPTER *Fourteen*

"Poor Breck..." sighed Frankie as she slid into the seat opposite Dylan. Alesha had made a quick exit once she'd seen that they had stuff to talk about. "He looked so hurt."

Dylan shrugged. "Well, he shouldn't go butting in where he's not wanted then." He flushed and then stared at his rapidly cooling fajitas, tonight's special.

"Oh," said Frankie. "Right." But although she was pleased that Dylan had broken his silence and unbelievably excited that he'd told Breck she was with *him* – and what did *that* mean? – she was angry too. She'd been having a really tough time and instead of being there for her, Dylan had disappeared like Sophie's bear. "So what's up then?" she muttered. "Why have you been avoiding me?"

Dylan fiddled with his knife and fork. "I'm sorry," he said. "I know that I've been…a bit, um… quiet since the snowboard cross. But I was a bit, well…jealous."

"Oh," said Frankie. "I see." She didn't really see at all. But she knew he was telling the truth and a little of her anger fizzled out. "So you've been acting like I'm invisible because of Breck," she said slowly. "Dylan, he's an idiot! I'm pretty sure he only tried to hook up with me because he wanted to show off in front of his friends. And he's really not my type."

"Yeah, I realize that now…" said Dylan, looking bashful. "But I got so *mad* when I saw him hugging you. And from where I was standing, it looked as if you were hugging him back, and I'd always hoped that after the Winter Olympics were over, Madame would lift her relationship ban and that, well, you'd be hugging *me*." He spoke the last words in a rush. By now, his cheeks were flaming redder than a stop light.

"Really?" whispered Frankie. She thought back to the Worlds, when she'd wished so hard that she'd win a gold medal at the Olympics *and* Dylan's heart. If he thought the same, then it would be a dream come true. But then she remembered Sophie and stiffened. What did Dylan have to say about *her*? She needed to find out.

"What is it?" asked Dylan.

"Ever since we arrived at the Olympic Village, you've been stuck to Sophie LaFleur like glue," she said, angrily. "I saw you hanging out with her at the Opening Ceremony party and then she was practically sitting on your lap on the bus. What's *that* all about?" She took a couple of deep breaths before continuing. "Dylan, you can't blame everything on Breck when you've been all over Sophie LaFleur. And I've been having a really tough time over Sophie's stupid bear… Where were *you*?"

Dylan stared at his plate and said nothing, while

Frankie slumped back in her seat, totally exhausted by her emotional outburst. As the seconds ticked by and the silence went on, she began to wonder if she'd gone too far. After all, Dylan wasn't the one who'd turned the entire figure-skating community against her – that was Sophie LaFleur.

"I'm *really* sorry, Frankie," Dylan said at last. "But Sophie wouldn't leave me alone. As soon as we arrived, she kept hanging around me, wanting to know my thoughts on everything from the Olympic rink to the taste of the chocolate here... You know, being generally friendly and cool? She can be really nice once you get to know her."

"Eh?" Frankie couldn't help sneering. Surely he was talking about some other Sophie LaFleur? This didn't sound *anything* like the Sophie that seemed to have been doing everything she could to sabotage Frankie's Olympic dream.

"I felt so jealous and cross when I saw you with Breck," Dylan went on. "Sophie flung her arms around me to make me feel better...just as you looked over." He grimaced. "That looked bad, right?"

Frankie nodded. "Really bad," she said. But she was starting to feel a little better. "*Why* didn't you talk to me about it…?" she asked.

He shrugged. "I'm an idiot," he said. "I tried to think of a way to apologize that wouldn't make me sound a complete fool. But I couldn't. And meanwhile, Sophie's been monopolizing my time. And if Sophie hasn't been hanging around me, Scarlett has. You'd think it'd be great to be in such demand… But it *really* isn't." He grinned wryly.

That should have quashed the last of Frankie's worries. Dylan had apologized and he'd explained everything. But there was just one more question she needed answering – something that had been niggling away at Frankie ever since the day of her short program. "How come you didn't wish me luck?" she whispered.

"But I *did*," protested Dylan, "just before you stepped onto the ice. Didn't you hear me?"

Dizzily, Frankie hurtled back to the day of the event and heard those softly spoken words again. *You can do it*, the voice had said. So it had been *Dylan* who she'd heard! Feelings of happiness and relief chased through her as, finally, she allowed herself to believe what he was saying. If only they'd spoken earlier, this silly misunderstanding could have been sorted out days ago... And all along, when she'd thought that she'd lost Dylan's friendship, it had been him who'd spurred her on to skate the best short program of her career.

"Thanks," she said.

"Is that all?" he teased, eyes twinkling. "Thanks?"

It was taking all of Frankie's concentration not to burst with excitement, but she managed a small nod. "Uh-huh."

"Well, I suppose that'll do for now," he said.

"Actually, there is one more thing," added Frankie.

Dylan's face was taut with concern once more. "What's that?"

"I think your dinner's cold."

Within minutes, it was as if the upset and nastiness of the last few days had never happened. The queue of athletes at the food counter ebbed and flowed as Frankie and Dylan talked non-stop about everything that had gone on since the night of the snowboard cross event. Dylan continued to apologize at regular intervals, until Frankie told him that if he didn't stop saying that he was sorry, she'd change her mind and sit with Breck instead.

"Sorry…" said Dylan, and then grimaced. "Oops."

Frankie rolled her eyes, but quickly became serious again. "About Breck…" she said. Ignoring Dylan's worried expression, she carried on. "It just doesn't ring true. Why did he search me out after he won gold? And then he behaved as if I was the loveliest creature he'd ever met. I never got the impression that even *he* believed that. I'm sure it was all an act."

Dylan didn't agree. "If he's been putting it on, then I'll skate to 'Bolero' in a tutu," he said. "So there."

At the thought of skating, Frankie's stomach did a double flip. She kept pushing tomorrow's main event to the back of her mind, but it was no good

– it just kept pinging back. She'd have to confront it soon, because in a little over twelve hours, she would be skating her free program. After more than two years of the toughest training, she'd have just four minutes to show the judges that she was the best of the best. And Frankie's Olympic-sized worry was that after her dismal performance at the rink this morning, she wouldn't be able to put one blade in front of the other.

"What's up?" Dylan asked gently.

Halting frequently to bite her lip or drum the table with nervous fingers, Frankie told him about the trip to the rink and how the negative vibes from Sophie's accusation had knocked her off her feet and destroyed the magic in her skating. "I'm afraid that I'm going to be a total flop tomorrow," she said. "What if I can't do it, Dylan?"

To Frankie's complete surprise, Dylan didn't look at all bothered by her confession. If anything, he looked as if he might laugh at her. Frankie's stomach did another flip. Didn't he care, after all? Totally numb, she watched as Dylan pushed his barely touched dinner to one side and leaned right across the table, before cupping her face in his hands.

"Listen to me," he said seriously, his eyes so close that Frankie could see the gold flecks in his gorgeously green eyes. "You are the best in the world," he said. "Madame knows it, Scarlett knows it, and I'm sure the nasty business with the mascot all kicked off because Sophie knows it too. And I've *always* known it. Go out there tomorrow and prove all of us right, okay?"

"B—" began Frankie.

But she didn't get the chance to say any more, because right there, in the middle of the canteen, with Olympic athletes whooping their approval all around, Dylan kissed her.

Wow.

If winning gold felt *this* amazing, then Frankie couldn't wait.

CHAPTER *Fifteen*

At last, tomorrow became today.

Today was the day of the Ladies' Free Program, the day that Frankie had looked forward to with excitement and dread in equal measure for *such* a long time. Today was the day that dreams might come true.

Or not.

But Frankie was trying not to think about *that*.

In fact, Frankie was trying very hard not to think about anything at all. She was concentrating on quelling the waves of nausea that rose in her throat as she sat in the changing room. Her right knee bounced up and down nervously. She thought of Mum, who must surely be here by now. Her flight times meant that there wasn't time for her to wish her daughter luck before she skated, but Frankie wasn't worried about that. She just wanted to make her mum proud. Frankie glanced at the clock. It wasn't long now.

Most of the other competitors had already skated, including Alesha, who had done way better than she herself had predicted…but sadly, not well enough to win a medal. She was now sitting beside Frankie, going over and over her routine.

"I lost it on the triple Axel, I *know* I did," Alesha said for the sixth time. "Overcooked it, totally. But you should have seen my layback spin…you know, the one that went into the Biellmann? I promise you that I didn't move even a millimetre from the spot! It was the best feeling in the world." She smiled bravely as Frankie squeezed her hand. "When are you on?"

"Last again…" sighed Frankie. She scanned the

changing room quickly. Now only a few of them remained. Sophie was plugged into her iPod in the corner, ignoring everyone else, while Alesha was keeping Frankie company. Marije Brom was there too, a beautiful blonde skater from the Netherlands who had been placed fifth after the short program. She was expected to do well.

"Good luck!" Frankie called after Marije, when it was her turn. She turned and grinned. Then, like characters on an old-fashioned clock, as Marije vanished, Scarlett appeared, flushed with excitement.

"I was *awesome*!" she screeched to the near-empty room, throwing her arms in the air and performing an impromptu jig, skates and all, before collapsing on the bench nearest Frankie and Alesha. "You should have *seen* me skate," she said. "I've won. I've *so* won. Seriously, it was the best performance of my career. I am *so* going to be a YouTube phenomenon by the end of the day. The television interviewer said that my routine was…dynamic and daring and graceful and…and…I'm *sure* there was something else…*dazzling*, that was it. He said I was dazzling!"

Frankie bit back the urge to comment that surely anyone whose outfit was covered in crystals could be described as "dazzling". But already, Scarlett had moved on to her scores. "Oh, silly me!" she squawked. "I didn't tell you how I did!"

"I'm guessing you did better than me...?" said Alesha softly.

"Duh," said Scarlett. "I'm only in the gold-medal position!" She spun round and started rooting around in her locker, missing the look of anguish that flew across Alesha's face. After a few seconds, she retrieved her designer handbag and plucked her mobile from inside. "I'm putting a photo of myself on my Facebook page right now," she announced. "Then my fans can see what an Olympic champion looks like!"

"Er...Scarlett," said Frankie, remembering something. "I thought Madame von Berne banned mobiles during the competition?"

"Goody-Two-Skates," scoffed Scarlett. "As if it's going to make *any* difference at all if I post a photo of myself. Although..." She peered at the glassy surface of her phone and sighed. "I thought as much. My lipgloss is totally gone. Too much smiling, I guess!" She plunged a hand into the bag again and this time retrieved a tube of lipgloss and a compact mirror from its depths.

While Scarlett was restoring her lips to their former shiny glory, Frankie grinned wryly to herself. She'd never met anyone quite like the Queen of the Ice and she suspected that she never would again. Undoubtedly talented, the other girl was so convinced that the gold medal belonged to her, she might as well be wearing it now. Self-absorbed, ultra-confident and completely selfish, Scarlett was unique. The only people she got along with were those who were willing to suck up to her 24–7. Anyone who promised to be anywhere near as good as Scarlett on the ice; anyone like Frankie... Well, they could forget it.

Click!

"Perfect," announced Scarlett as she studied the photo she'd taken with her iPhone. Frowning slightly, she peered closer at the screen.

"Something wrong?" Alesha said in a bored voice. "Spinach in your teeth? Are you wearing last year's shade of lipgloss by mistake?"

Scarlett didn't seem to hear her. With speed she usually reserved for the ice, she leaped up and, still wearing her figure skates, shot across to Sophie with an ungainly hoppity-skip action, coming to a dead halt in front of her.

"What do you think you're—?" began Sophie. Her cheeks flushed, she seemed to be fumbling with something.

"Shouldn't I be asking *you* that?" demanded Scarlett. "I can see you quite clearly in the background of my photo. You look as if you are holding something. What is it?"

"What are you bleating on about?" groaned Frankie. Clearly, something had got Scarlett riled, but couldn't she have postponed her outburst until *after* Frankie's free program? But, of course, she didn't care about that. That was the problem, wasn't it? As far as Scarlett was concerned, everything was *always* about her. Neither Sophie nor Frankie had skated yet. Why was Scarlett winding them up before the competition? Bristling with anger, Frankie leaped to her feet. "Hey, Scarlett!" she shouted. "I'm competing for Olympic gold in ten minutes. It's the biggest event of my *life*. I'm supposed to be preparing myself, *not* watching you doing an impression of the paparazzi. Why can't you think of other people for a change?"

Scarlett whirled round and glared furiously at her. "That's what I *am* doing, Frankie," she growled.

Frankie shrank back from the other girl's anger. But then she steeled herself for confrontation. She'd waited too long. Over two years, she'd been at the Ice Palace with Scarlett, and in that time she'd let the other girl walk all over her. Whenever she'd had the chance, Scarlett had made nasty comments, poked fun at her and repeatedly tried to get her into trouble. Well, she'd had enough. And then... Frankie's eyes flicked towards Sophie and – *bam!* – her anger at Scarlett vanished.

There, in Sophie's hands, was a small cuddly toy. It was Barney the bear.

Glaring first at Scarlett and then at Frankie, Sophie's lip curled into a scornful sneer. "You can try to prove it," she said, "but I bet you can't see *anything* in that photo. Everyone thinks you stole it, Frankie. I'm the local hero and you're the thief. It's going to take a lot to change people's minds about that." She smiled nastily. "The damage is already done."

"Let's see about that," said Scarlett. Before Sophie had time to react, she lunged towards her.

"Scarlett, *don't!*" cried Frankie, dragging her away.

Sophie took her chance. Before anyone could stop her, she stuffed the mascot into her locker, slammed shut the metal door and flicked the lock.

"Too late!" trilled Sophie. "See ya!" Neatly dodging around a furious Scarlett, she ran towards the exit as quickly as her figure skates would allow. By the door, she paused, adding, "Do excuse me. I've got a gold medal to win." Then she was gone.

There was a stunned silence.

Frankie gulped. She didn't know what was scarier: the thought of taking part in the Olympic Games or apologizing to Scarlett. She'd been *so* wrong about her. Not only had Scarlett busted Sophie, she'd stood up for Frankie too. Wow.

Frankie took a deep breath. "Scarlett," she said. "I'm sorry. I thought you were going to hit her—"

"Oh, put a sock in it," snapped Scarlett. "That's not my style. I was going to seize the evidence, you *idiot*. And if you hadn't stopped me, you'd be off the hook. Now all I've got is this long-distance shot of some weird, fluffy thing. *Well done.*"

Frankie pressed her lips together in a grim smile and swallowed the apology. Scarlett might have done her a favour, but there was no danger of them ever being friends – either on the ice or off it.

Things were back to normal.

Chapter *Sixteen*

Events in the changing room were interrupted by a long rumble of applause and a few muffled whoops from the other side of the double doors. Fear coursed through Frankie as she realized what was happening in the vast Olympic stadium. Marije Brom had now finished her routine, which meant that there were only two skaters left to compete: Sophie and Frankie herself.

Once Scarlett had flounced out of the changing room, Frankie slumped onto the bench and put her head in her hands. She'd ruined Scarlett's plan *and* she'd offended her at the same time. But worst of all, Frankie's concentration was shot to pieces.

"I can't skate like this…" she wailed.

"You're right," Alesha agreed. "You've still got your guards on your blades. You'd fall over in no time."

Against her will, Frankie smiled.

"That's better," said Alesha firmly, but her dark eyes were filled with concern as she crouched down to speak directly to her. "Frankie, please listen to me. There's going to be heaps of time to sort out the nasty business with Sophie afterwards. Now, you have to focus on the free skate."

Frankie took a couple of deep breaths, knowing that Alesha was right.

"So, come on," Alesha said, tugging Frankie to her feet. "You're not going to feel any better by sitting here. No arguments. We're not going to watch Sophie's routine on TV. We're going to watch it *live*. If she skates a blinder, then at least you'll know about it and you can up your game. Know your enemy, that's what they say, right?"

Feeling sick with nerves, Frankie gave a small nod. She couldn't think of anything she'd like less. But she also knew that deep down, she was dying to get out there and get on with it. Surely the reality couldn't be any worse than the fear she felt waiting backstage? "All right," she said reluctantly.

Alesha caught hold of Frankie's hand and pulled her gently towards the stadium, still holding on tightly as they pushed through the double doors, as if worried that she might make a run for it.

Frankie felt her breathing quicken as they emerged from the changing room and followed the route into the competitors' area of the stadium. Her view was blocked by hoardings, but as they waited for Marije's scores to be announced, the low rumble of thousands of voices seemed to make the air vibrate with unseen energy. This place had been buzzing on the day of the short program, but today the atmosphere was totally *electric*. Frankie felt better already. And then she emerged from behind the hoardings and saw the stadium.

"Wow."

Perhaps she hadn't taken it all in on the day of

the short programs, but today Frankie's eyes widened as she stared and stared, almost staggering backwards at the sight. The huge Olympic stadium was filled to capacity, the spectator seats a sea of constantly moving colour. Flags – from very small to tablecloth-size – were waved aloft, Union flags dotted among them, held by fans who'd travelled thousands of miles to support Team GB.

Slowly, Frankie made her way past the skaters and coaches who lined the benches. They were all staring at the vast stadium too, as if mesmerized. As for Frankie, she felt awestruck, terrified and unbearably excited, all at the same time. It felt so different from the last time she'd skated here.

Last time, she hadn't been one routine away from a medal.

Now, she was.

Over in the kiss-and-cry area, Frankie could see Marije Brom systematically chewing each one of her fingernails as she awaited her scores. Frankie hadn't seen the girl's routine, so she had no idea how she'd done, but as the results were read out over the PA system, she realized that although they were good, they weren't good enough to win. Marije's shoulders slumped just a fraction as the last score was announced and her slim chance of a medal vanished with it, but she wiped away a quick tear and kept smiling. Frankie joined in the tumultuous applause for the other girl.

As she was staring, Frankie noticed Scarlett not far away. She appeared to be in deep discussion with Madame von Berne, who was nodding intently.

"Hey," said a low voice.

Frankie tore her attention away from Madame and Scarlett and saw Dylan sitting on one of the benches. "What are *you* doing here?" she asked, joining him and making room for Alesha too. "I'm not sure you're entered in the ladies' competition, are you…?"

"Nah." Dylan gave her his trademark grin and despite her nerves, she couldn't help smiling back. "It's a better view from here," he said. "Besides, I wanted to wish you luck before your routine."

"Thanks," she murmured. This time, she knew that she definitely had Dylan's support and it gave her a wonderfully warm glow.

"What's been going on back there?" he asked suddenly. "In the changing room, I mean. First, Sophie shot out as if she'd been fired from a cannon. And then Scarlett came racing after her. Was there a catfight or something?"

"Er...something like that," admitted Frankie, glancing towards the kiss-and-cry area. Now there was no sign of either Madame or Scarlett. "Tell you later," she said. There wasn't time to explain everything at the moment. Besides, if she started thinking again about how Sophie had deliberately tried to blacken her name, she was going to get really mad. And right now, with the most important moment of her life hurtling towards her like a runaway train, that *really* wasn't a good idea.

Dylan nodded. "Okay," he said softly.

Flashing him a grateful smile, Frankie turned her attention towards the ice. It stretched emptily away from her – an expanse of gleaming silvery-white waiting to be filled with the performance of a lifetime. Could she do it? And even if she could, would it be enough to win...? Frankie squeezed her eyes shut and tried to run through her routine one more time. But she could get no further than the first jump. Panic coursed through her. What came after that? *What came next?* What if she couldn't remember when she got out on the ice? What if—?

"And now," boomed the PA, "we have Sophie LaFleur from Canada!"

Frankie felt as if someone had poured a bucket of freezing-cold water over her. Eyes wide open now, she stared as Sophie briefly hugged her coach before stepping onto the ice to resounding cheers from the huge audience. Valentine Dubois watched her go, her face a mask of steely determination.

"Rumour has it, she'll do anything to make sure Sophie wins," said Dylan in a low voice. "All the gossips reckon that Sophie is her last chance to get her hands on a gold medal. She never won one herself, you see."

"Oh," said Frankie. She knew this, of course. Madame von Berne had told her as much. So why was it bugging her now? Whatever – now wasn't the time to be sorting out rinkside politics because, with a gentle cascade of musical notes, Sophie's instrumental piece started, neatly putting an end to Frankie's tortured thoughts. She settled back in her seat. The only thing she could do now was watch.

The music was an excellent choice, ideally suited to the fluid movements that Sophie performed with effortless ease. A series of incredible jumps soon had the crowd cheering for more and as the tempo of the music increased, changing into an upbeat pop tune, Sophie played to her audience, delighting them with a perfect flying sit spin and a stunning triple flip. She stumbled slightly on the exit from the move, but swiftly recovered her poise and moved on to an exquisite layback spin.

Frankie had watched every major championship since, well, for ever. But she'd never seen anything like this. Put quite simply, the other girl was as near perfection as she'd ever seen. Without the stumble, it would have *been* perfect.

But while Sophie's routine progressed towards its stunning conclusion – a swirling, whirling collection of jumps and spins that seemed to cover almost every millimetre of the huge rink, Frankie spotted something strange out of the corner of her eye. The two Madames – von Berne and Dubois – were having the most heated row she'd ever seen. As she watched, angrily mouthed phrases flew back and forth. Their arms waved so vigorously that they looked like overexcited traffic controllers. And then a man joined them – tall and dark, with greying temples. He looked familiar, but Frankie couldn't place him. Where had she seen him before? A vague memory nagged at her, but remained annoyingly out of reach. With a heavy frown bunching his dark brow, the man began to speak to the two coaches, who glared at him. But their argument seemed to have cooled a little and after a few tense seconds, Valentine Dubois stalked away. Wearing a look of victory, Madame watched her go. Then she turned to the very handsome older man and smiled at him.

What was going on?

Maddeningly, there wasn't time for Frankie to find out. She looked back towards the rink to see that Sophie was wowing the delighted audience with a final spin. Then it was over and she was bowing repeatedly as wave after wave of applause rolled around the vast stadium. Bunches of flowers skittered across the ice towards her feet. Smiling graciously, the Canadian girl bent to retrieve them and at last, when it seemed that the clapping and cheering might go on for ever, she skated slowly from the ice. A group of skaters hastily sped around the rink, gathering the many bouquets that Sophie LaFleur hadn't been able to carry.

It was as Sophie walked regally into the kiss-and-cry area – hugging and kissing her coach, her parents and anyone who could get near enough en route – that Frankie finally admitted the truth to herself.

And in her heart of hearts, she'd known it all along.

Sophie had won.

Chapter *Seventeen*

The hordes of news reporters, camera operators and photographers swooped towards Sophie LaFleur, each of them eager to witness the moment when her scores were announced.

Gracefully, Sophie LaFleur sat down on the bench in the kiss-and-cry area, smiling at each of the onlookers in turn. Madame Valentine Dubois joined her, putting a proprietorial arm around the figure skater's shoulders and adding her own confident smile to Sophie's.

"I'd better get going," Frankie whispered in Dylan's ear. "I know there isn't really any point me skating now, not after that performance, but—"

"What do you *mean*?" Dylan demanded.

Shocked by his tone, Frankie looked at Dylan and was astonished at what she saw. His green eyes sparked and his cheeks were flushed with anger. He was completely furious. "What?" she asked, shrinking back a little. Frankie had *never* seen him look this mad.

"There is *every* point in you skating," Dylan told her, speaking slowly and deliberately. He seemed to be having difficulty keeping his voice down and it trembled with suppressed anger. "Weren't you listening to me last night? You can skate better than every person competing today," he said. He glanced briefly and apologetically towards Alesha, who was listening in stunned silence. "Sorry, Alesha," he said. "No offence."

"None taken," Alesha said lightly.

Dylan turned back to Frankie. "You just don't get it, do you?" he said, shaking his head in disbelief. "You light up the ice like no one I've ever seen.

Technically, you're amazing, but it's more than that…" He paused, as if searching for the right words and then his lips curved into the most fabulous smile, his anger fading. "Don't you see, Frankie? You're a *natural*. Just like Madame told you after she first watched you skate."

"Oh," Frankie said. She felt buffeted. She felt stunned. She felt *great*. And as she stared back at Dylan, a wave of excitement washed over her and she began to smile. "Do you really think I can do it?" she asked, just to be sure that she hadn't imagined Dylan's splendid outburst.

"No," he replied, solemnly shaking his head.

Her heart sank. "Oh."

"I *know* you can do it," he said, his eyes twinkling now.

"I'm sorry to interrupt," said Alesha, "but so do I. Know you can do it, I mean. You're a winner, Frankie."

Frankie flung her arms around them both. "Thank you so much," she murmured into Dylan's Team GB sweatshirt.

"Now, stop being an idiot and go and win a gold

medal," Dylan told her with mock sternness.

"I'll do my best," said Frankie. Taking a slightly shaky breath, she headed towards the waiting area, where she could already see Madame von Berne tapping her foot impatiently.

"*There* you are," said the coaching director, looking more anxious than Frankie had ever seen her. "You're on as soon as Sophie's marks are in. Now sit down and wait here."

Frankie nodded. Then she stared in amazement as Madame hurried away. Where was she going? And why was she going there *now*? Frankie sighed and turned her attention back to the scoreboard. She would *never* understand Madame.

The judges seemed to be taking an awfully long time to decide how to score Sophie's routine. Trying not to panic, Frankie sat down and smoothed her fingers down the silvery fabric of her skirt. She was wearing quite the most beautiful dress she'd ever seen – either off the ice or on it. Stefan, Team GB's brilliant one-man wardrobe department, had created a dress so dazzling that even Scarlett Jones had been silent when she'd first seen it.

The dress was asymmetric. The neckline was slashed diagonally from the shoulder, which meant that the dress was long-sleeved on one side and sleeveless on the other. The fabric tapered in at the waist, before fanning out into a short skirt that was also asymmetric – longer on the left, shorter on the right. But it was the fabric that was stunning. Stefan had found a beautiful rose-pink organza and he'd covered this with so many tiny silver sequins that from a distance it almost seemed to glow.

The beautiful dress made Frankie feel like a real Ice Princess, just as she'd always longed to be. Now she just had to skate like one.

The scores were in.

And they were *so* good.

Sophie's total had been boosted to 230, which was the highest combined score in the ladies' competition this year. But that wasn't all. It wasn't just the best result this year…it was the best result in the ladies' figure skating in the entire history of the Winter Olympics.

In other words, it was totally unbeatable.

Frankie felt the gold medal slipping from her

grasp once more. With such phenomenal marks, she knew, even if no one else did, that it was going to be impossible to beat her rival. She watched Sophie on one of the screens dotted around the stadium. The other girl was now beaming widely and waiting for her first question from the assembled press.

"Well done! You must be thrilled with that score," one of the interviewers said to Sophie. "Especially after the nasty business after the short program, I mean. I'm sure everyone is delighted that you managed to skate so well after all – *without* your lucky mascot, I mean." He held out the microphone for her reply.

Sophie's winning smile faded just a little. "We-e-ell," she began. "The thing is—"

Madame Dubois cut in quickly. "We've just had some tremendous news," she said, beaming like a toothpaste advert. "The mascot wasn't taken at all. Sophie simply mislaid Barney and now she's simply delighted to have found him again."

A strange thought occurred to Frankie. What if the problem wasn't Sophie at all? What if someone had told Sophie to make up the story about the theft? The same person who'd had a go at Frankie in the cable car? Had they also told Sophie to make a play for Dylan? And to cannon into Frankie at the rink? Had Madame von Berne been right to suspect Madame Dubois? She remembered their discussion in the coffee shop and how Madame had said they were once rivals. In fact, was *Madame Valentine Dubois* to blame for every mean thing that had happened to Frankie since she'd arrived at the Olympics?

The interviewer looked slightly perplexed. "So, let me get this straight. This means that you *don't* have an enemy after all, Sophie?" he said. "No one stole your mascot?"

"Er...that's right," replied Sophie, looking confused and more than a little angry. But she recovered her poise almost at once and laughingly explained to the press that it had all been a silly mistake. "Would you believe that it was at the back of my locker all the time?" she said. Her eyes were wide and innocent, her face wreathed in smiles.

Frankie was speechless. She was *totally* off the

hook, which meant that the suspicious looks, the snide comments and the muttered conversations of the last few days would all stop. The feeling of relief was unbelievable. But unanswered questions remained. Why had Madame Dubois chosen to tell viewers about the mascot? And why had she done it *now*, when the whole world was watching? Frankie stared at her arch-rival's coach, trying to work it out. And that was when she caught the angry look that Valentine Dubois was giving someone. Frankie flinched at the suppressed rage she saw in the woman's eyes, even though she knew that it wasn't aimed at her. She was too far away. No, as Frankie stared across the rink to where the interview was taking place, she saw that the object of Madame Dubois's rage must be Team GB's coaching director, who was now standing just off-camera. So that was where she'd gone in such a hurry.

Frankie frowned.

But there was no time to work it out, because officials were shooing the press away and Madame was pushing her way around the rink to where

Frankie was sitting and gently pulling her to her feet, propelling her student in the direction of the rink. "Focus, Frankie," she whispered. "Everyone knows that you're innocent now. Keep that thought and forget the rest. All you have to do is skate."

"But—?" began Frankie.

Madame shook her head. "Explanations can wait. Go and show everyone what a star you are." She grasped Frankie by the shoulders and stared right at her. Usually, the coach's blue eyes were icy cold and expressionless. Now, they were filled with indescribable emotion. "*Skate to win, Frankie*," she whispered. "You're not going for the silver medal. You're going for *gold*."

Frankie gulped and gave the tiniest of nods. She shut her eyes and suddenly everything became pin sharp. It didn't matter what was going on outside the rink, whether it was Sophie's U-turn or Valentine Dubois's weird looks, because none of it had *anything* to do with what went on *on the ice*. Frankie was fed up of people messing with her head. She was fed up of them trying to blame her, upset her and trip her up. But no more.

Determinedly, she pushed all of the stupid, troublesome, petty things that had plagued her out of her mind, until only one thing remained…

And that was her free skate. It had to be brilliant.

Frankie opened her eyes.

"Our next competitor represents Great Britain," boomed the PA. *"Ladies and gentlemen, a warm welcome please for Frankie Wills!"*

Frankie paused. She'd trained so hard, practised this routine a million times. But now it was for real. Only the most fabulous skating would get her onto the winners' podium.

"Come on, Frankie!" cried the voice that had read her a thousand bedtime stories. It was *Mum.* She grinned, unbelievably pleased to hear her, even if she couldn't see her. And then she focused again.

Frankie stepped onto the ice.

This was it.

CHAPTER *Eighteen*

It was like entering the most bizarre dream ever.

As Frankie glided forward, the sounds of the crowd faded and then even the spectators themselves blurred and seemed to vanish completely. All that remained was the gentle rasp of blade on ice and the coolness of the air that rushed by her ears as she skated. As if by magic, her nerves had evaporated, leaving behind a sense of utter calm. She swooped towards the centre of the rink, coming to a halt with a precise one-footed stop. Slowly, she raised her arms, placed her left toe pick on the ice. And then she waited to start the routine that would either win her a medal – or lose her one.

For a few seconds, there was utter silence as Frankie waited for the music to begin. It was a dazzling sequence of excerpts from West End shows. All had been chosen by Frankie for no other reason than the fact that she loved them and knew instinctively that they would inspire her to skate her very best. The sound engineer had mixed the pieces of music into a four-minute track that started fast, slowed for a magically dreamy middle section, before powering up into a fabulous finale. Her routine was built around the medley, perfectly timed to accompany the notes to the second.

With a crash of cymbals, the music began.

Taking a deep breath, Frankie swept her right foot in a large arc, pivoting in a circle before curving into a graceful camel spin and then seamlessly reversing her direction with a three-turn, before accelerating away with smooth back crossovers. She gathered her strength for the first combination jump, leaping into the air with a fabulous triple

Lutz and briefly touching down, before launching into a triple toe-loop and landing with a gentle *dink*.

Phew. Frankie knew instinctively that the first of the jump combinations in her routine was completely perfect.

Perhaps the thousands of spectators clapped… she didn't have a clue. Everything in her being was focused on the softly glistening ice as she expertly spun and whirled and danced across the rink towards her triple Salchow, making every move count. She knew that the judges weren't just looking for big show-off jumps – they were looking for smooth transitions too. And good footwork, difficult turns, speed, variety…the list went on. *Everything* had to be just right.

The triple Salchow was stunning.

The sit spin was faultless.

And then Frankie was surging onwards to the next jump, her entire body tingling with excitement as she leaped skyward into the best triple Axel of her life. She couldn't have stopped skating now, even if she'd wanted to.

And then came the triple Lutz.

Frankie went into the three-turn as usual and then her right foot jolted. Whether it was a dip in the surface or a chunk of loose ice was unclear, but whatever it was, it threw her off-balance. Big time. Instinctively, Frankie realized that if she performed the jump now, it would go wrong. No question. And a poorly executed jump or bodged landing would cost her dearly. Thinking quickly, she realized that there was only one choice to make – she skipped the jump, filling the gap with an extra mohawk and, to regain her poise, a triple flip.

Now the pressure was on. Frankie's freestyle routine already included the maximum number of jump combinations – three, in all. There wasn't space in the program to squeeze in another combination. No, she had to come up with another idea.

But what?

It was as she headed for the next element – a bent-leg layover camel spin, also known as a Yu-Na spin – that Frankie realized how she could do it. The double flip, triple toe-loop and double loop combination in her routine was tricky, but if she could pull off a *triple* flip instead of a double, then it just might transform it from tricky to fiendishly difficult, and win her the extra points she needed. The combination was near the end of the entire routine, so there was still time for her to change her mind. Right now, though, it was the Yu-Na spin that she had to concentrate on. Frankie whirled round and round, focusing fully on holding her free leg aloft. And then, after a quick change of direction, she sped onwards to the next move.

The music had slowed and Frankie's moves followed suit. With a fluidity learned during countless hours of training with the indomitable Madame, she changed edges again and again, swerving this way and that, peppering her routine with the hops, spins and spirals that she hoped would impress the judges as much as her jumps.

The flip jump loomed closer. The tempo of the music increased again and Frankie was in the final section of her routine. Closer…and closer… And then it was time to make her mind up. Should she take a wild chance and go for the triple or should she stick to the routine she knew and lose the chance to improve her score…?

Frankie had no choice.

It had to be another triple.

She began with a mohawk turn, keeping her right free leg low and straight with her weight over the other foot. Her left arm was in front of her body, the right arm behind and her skating knee bent. She was ready.

Pushing off with her right foot, Frankie pulled both arms down strongly…and then up and in sharply towards her body, knowing that the speed and strength of her movements would make all the difference. Triple jumps didn't take longer to do than doubles. That was the problem with gravity – it had a habit of pulling skaters back down to earth. Triples were just faster. A *lot* faster. So, in the air, Frankie kept her arms crossed tighter than tight across her chest, elbows firmly down. Her left leg was crossed lightly over her right. She spun once… twice…could she do it…? Yes! *Three times!* It was a textbook landing. And with barely time to catch her breath, Frankie went straight into the triple toe-loop… *Phew*. She landed it. But she couldn't relax yet, because she had to finish the combination. Her energy running dangerously low after the punishing jumps, she went for the third – the double loop. She leaped, spinning quickly and tightly, knowing that all rotation must be completed before she touched down…

Could she make it? Or had she just done the most foolish thing in the entire history of figure skating and exchanged the wonderfully shiny silver medal that she was on track to win, for no medal at all?

Down…down…down… Bending her knee low to absorb the impact, Frankie landed *perfectly*.

And as she did so, a faint noise began to sound in her ears. It persisted all the way through the dizzying I-spin that ended her routine…and beyond. Gradually, it became louder and louder. And as Frankie slowed to a halt, she finally realized what the sound was.

It was the sound of the crowd.

Curiously absent for the duration of Frankie's routine, the spectators now pinged back into focus.

And they were much, much noisier than they had been before. The vast stadium rang with the resounding cheers of thousands of delighted people. One by one, they rose from their seats until every last one of them was standing. They clapped and shouted and stamped their feet so loudly that, to begin with, Frankie was puzzled. She was the last competitor – had she been so focused on her routine that she'd missed an important announcement about the event?

"*Frankieeeeeee!*" cried a deliriously happy voice that somehow managed to rise above the noise. "You *star!*"

It was when she saw Alesha, hanging over the barrier and waving madly at her, that Frankie finally realized what was going on. The cheers were for *her*, Frankie Wills. The spectators at least seemed to think that she'd done well. As she watched the flowers that bounced and skidded across the ice and skated stiffly to collect them, Frankie began to smile. She didn't know if she'd skated well enough to win, but for now, it was enough to know that the audience loved it.

Her arms filled with white roses, Frankie performed a clumsy curtsy, easily the clunkiest and least accomplished move of her entire performance.

But nobody seemed to mind.

In fact, they carried on clapping as if they'd never stop.

Chapter *Nineteen*

It was seriously the best thing ever.

As Frankie listened to the cheers and whoops that continued to surge around the massive arena long after the music stopped, she knew that she'd never felt so good. The totally unreal feeling that had taken over as she had first stepped onto the ice persisted now, making everything seem so much brighter and more colourful than normal. Flashlights from a thousand cameras sparkled in the crowd. It was like being in a movie.

"Wow…" she murmured to herself. "Just, wow."

Frankie had no idea how long she remained on the ice, skating to each corner of the arena in turn, curtsying over and over to the wildly applauding spectators. But there was one thing that she was very sure about – she loved every magical millisecond of it. Later, Alesha proudly told her that the standing ovation lasted for a record-breaking five minutes and twelve seconds. Right now, it seemed timeless.

When she stepped from the ice and into the kiss-and-cry area at last, Frankie was glowing with happiness. She looked for someone – *anyone* – that she recognized, but there were just well-wishers, officials and new fans, all clamouring to meet her. These weren't the people she wanted to see…

"Where *is* everyone?" Frankie murmured. And then she spotted a familiar face, weaving her way towards Frankie, wearing quite the biggest smile she'd ever seen. Frankie did a double take. But when she looked back, it really *was* Madame Kristiana von Berne.

"I *knew* you could do it," said the Team GB coaching director, her eyes glistening with tears.

"But you were even better than I hoped. Your performance was…was…" She stopped and sniffed loudly, displaying more emotion in a few seconds than Frankie had seen in two and a half years. "It was *perfect*," she managed at last. "*Just perfect.*" And she flung her arms around Frankie and hugged her.

"Er…thank you," breathed Frankie. Then her heart sank as she remembered the triple flip. Perhaps Madame hadn't noticed her mistake. Well, she'd see it on the reruns, so it was best if Frankie admitted it now. "I'm really sorry," she began, "but I missed the—"

Madame cut her off almost at once with an airy wave of her manicured fingers. "The triple Lutz?" she said. "Dear girl, don't worry about *that*. I saw that the ice was uneven and you made by far the most sensible decision in the circumstances. Besides, you made up for it later, didn't you? *More* than made up for it with that magnificent combination with the extra rotation in the flip jump. Pure *genius*." She took Frankie's hand and squeezed it, looking her right in the eyes. "Believe me, there have not been many times when I've described something as *perfect*, but this is one of them. You were *wonderful* out there."

"Thank you," said Frankie, bashfully. Praise from Madame was virtually unheard of. But she was saved the trouble of further comment by Alesha, who burst through the crowd in a flurry of squeals and frantic arm-waving.

"You were awesome!" Alesha cried, throwing herself at Frankie so hard that she almost toppled her. She enveloped Frankie in a huge bear hug.

"Have you seen my mum?" gasped Frankie. It was fabulous to find Alesha, but she *so* wanted Mum to be here too.

Alesha shrugged. "Sorry," she said apologetically. "This crowd's so big, I don't think I could find Torvill and Dean dressed up in their Bolero costumes in it. The chances of spotting your mum are zero."

"And where's Dylan?" mumbled Frankie. She so wanted to know what *he* thought of her routine.

"Stuck in the crush with Paul," explained Alesha. She stepped back, still grinning widely. "I trod on a few toes to get here. I expect he's being more polite."

"Yeah, that must be it…" murmured Frankie, scanning the crowd for him. And then she saw him. Her heart plummeted. Dylan *wasn't* struggling through the hordes of officials to congratulate her. He was half-hidden behind Sophie LaFleur. What could *she* be saying to him? Suddenly, as Frankie worked out what was going on, she didn't feel quite so wonderful any more. Sophie was trying to influence Dylan before Frankie could expose her lies… And as she stared in astonishment, Breck appeared, all smiles. What was *he* doing there?

"Frankie?" Madame said gently. "The judges are ready to announce your scores."

Numbly, Frankie tore her gaze away from the unlikely trio and sat down with the coaching director on the hard benches where everyone waited to receive their scores. Now it was her turn. With the cameras on her, Frankie did her best to smile and not to fidget. What did it matter about Dylan anyway? What was any boy compared to the dazzling achievement of a medal? Perhaps Madame von Berne had been right all along. Forget Dylan and romantic attachments and concentrate on figure skating. That's what she'd told her *so* many times.

Now, Frankie was going to do just that. She lifted her chin and smiled for all she was worth.

"Here we go…" said Madame.

Her pulse racing, Frankie tried to listen to the scores. But she couldn't take anything in. Nervous beyond belief, now she was this close to a gold medal, Frankie wanted to win so badly that it hurt.

There was an interminable pause.

"*Which means that, with a final combined score of 233…*"

Frankie held her breath.

"*…the winner of the Olympic ladies' figure skating gold is…*"

What had Sophie scored? Frankie racked her brains, but she couldn't remember. The pause went on. Could they drag this out any longer? Frankie felt sure she was about to turn into a fossil, she'd been waiting here so long. She glanced quickly at Madame von Berne. The coach was smiling.

"...*Frankie Wills of Great Britain!*"

The world stood still.

And then, as deafening cheers began to sound all around, Frankie realized that it was true, really true. She had won gold, three points ahead of Sophie LaFleur, who was doing her best to look thrilled about the silver. Poor Scarlett – and right now, Frankie really did feel sorry for Scarlett, because she knew just how fabulous it felt to win a medal – had been nudged into fourth place by Russian skater, Olga Krugalov, who'd won bronze by the narrowest of margins.

And then the huge crowd of spectators, everyone around Frankie – even the TV reporters, who were poised ready to interview her – *all* of them went mad. Frankie felt herself swept from her feet and squeezed in the most amazing hug and she squealed gleefully. Clearly, she had a very enthusiastic fan. She looked up to see who it was and found herself staring right at Dylan. He was smiling as if *he'd* just won gold, not her.

Frankie beamed at him. And then...she stopped and drew back slightly as she remembered what she'd just witnessed. "What were you doing with Sophie?" she asked.

"I was telling her that I'm with *you*," said Dylan, presenting her with a slightly dishevelled bunch of sunflowers. "You're the one I want, Frankie," he whispered, so only she could hear. "Not Sophie or anyone else, but you. It's *always* been you."

And right in front of the TV cameras, which were relaying events *live* to an audience of millions, he kissed her.

If Frankie had thought that the day was already full of surprises, it was about to get a whole lot more surprising…because Dylan wasn't the only one to astound her.

First, she fielded questions from the world's press.

"*How does it feel to be an Olympic champion?*"

Frankie grinned. "Amazing."

"*What was your favourite part of the routine?*"

That was easy. "The extra rotation that I squeezed in to boost my scores, no question."

"*What are you going to do next?*"

At this, she shrugged and smiled. "Admire my gold medal, of course," she said, to the amusement of the interviewer.

"Well done, Frankie," said the woman from the BBC. "You deserved to win."

Madame von Berne, who had been hovering in the background now pulled her pupil aside. "Take a moment to prepare yourself for the ceremony," she said. "Believe me, it'll be a moment to cherish for the rest of your life." The coach had been smiling for twelve minutes solid, which Frankie privately figured must be a record.

Frankie grinned back. She glanced quickly over to the rink, where officials were preparing the podium for the medal ceremony. They still had a few minutes to wait. She bit her lip thoughtfully. Did she dare? Yes, she decided. She did. "The thing is…" Frankie said, "I wondered what happened to make Sophie confess the truth about the lucky mascot. Because that really helped to boost my confidence before I skated. Do you have any idea why…?"

Madame gave her a sidelong glance, as if perfectly aware that Frankie guessed she had something to do with it. "It's quite straightforward," she said. "I think you know already that Scarlett took a photo of herself and that Sophie happened to be in the background," she said. "With Barney the bear."

Frankie nodded.

"Well, as I'm sure you know, it was a terrible shot. Sophie could have been holding *anything*." For a second, the coaching director looked a little guilty. "So I'm afraid that I called Madame Dubois's bluff. I told her that we actually had a very clear image – absolute proof that Barney was not stolen."

Frankie just stared. She couldn't help thinking that if Madame von Berne hadn't been a figure skater or a coach, she would have made an awesome double agent.

"Valentine Dubois admitted everything at once," Madame continued. "It turns out that she put Sophie up to it. And the silly girl agreed. I told Valentine that unless she revealed the truth before you skated then I would have no choice but to report her to the International Olympic Committee, which may have resulted in an unfortunate disqualification." She gave a brief shrug and half-turned back to the rink, where the podium was nearing completion. "So, Valentine and Sophie have confessed, the photo will be deleted and, next time, Scarlett will follow the rules and leave her mobile at home. I hope that clears everything up?"

"Er…not *really*," said Frankie. Deep down, she knew there was more to it. Frankie knew from Madame that she and Valentine went way back. They obviously weren't friends now, so what had happened between them? No, unless Frankie was very much mistaken, there was a *lot* more to be cleared up.

Madame kept her voice low. "You already know that Valentine Dubois and I fought over a medal, many years ago," she said. The coach paused and seemed to steel herself before continuing, as if it hurt her to speak. "I injured myself and never skated again. Valentine simply wasn't good enough. And she couldn't deal with that. Her revenge was to steal something – *someone* – that I loved very much. My coach made us split up, but Valentine made sure that we never got back together. And, it's pretty fair to say that I was heartbroken…" The coaching director stopped and all at once she looked unbearably sad.

"Oh," said Frankie. She didn't know what else *to* say. Finally, the last pieces of the jigsaw slotted into place. So Valentine Dubois had stolen the boy that Madame had loved. Frankie felt desperately sorry for the Team GB coach. It was so unfair.

"Now," said Madame, abruptly back to her totally businesslike self. "If you could keep that to yourself, I'd be *very* grateful." She smiled sweetly as a photographer swooped towards them.

Frankie smiled automatically. She'd been granted a brief glimpse of the real Madame, but now it was over… Then something made her look up and she caught her breath. Dodging through the crowd towards them was the man she'd seen talking to Madame and Valentine Dubois – the man who'd seemed strangely familiar. In a flash, Frankie knew exactly where she'd seen him. This was the same man who Madame had been talking to at the ice rink the other day. Could *this* be the man who had gone off with Valentine Dubois and broken Madame's heart? Frankie watched as he approached the coaching director and gently took her hand.

"Isn't that Viktor Schilling?" someone behind her asked. "He was a marvellous skater in his day. Took gold in the 1982 World Championships, didn't he?"

Frankie grinned. Was the coaching director going to get a happy ending too? She did hope so. Madame deserved to be as happy as she was – and it might put her in a better mood back at Skate School too!

Then there was a strange lull as the crowd quietened and it was far too late to find out.

"Frankie!" Dylan called urgently. "They're waiting for you!"

"*Already?*" cried Frankie. And all thoughts of everything except the gold medal flew from her mind. With trembling fingers, she pulled the guards from her figure-skate blades and stepped onto the silvery ice.

Chapter *Twenty*

"*Stop!*"

Frankie looked up in surprise. Scarlett Jones was dodging through the crowds towards the barrier. At the last minute she slowed, so that by the time she reached Frankie, she was sauntering nonchalantly, as if she had all the time in the world.

"Scarlett!" said Frankie. She'd forgotten all about her, but there was something she really needed to say to the girl who'd been her biggest rival ever since she'd arrived at Skate School. "I want to thank you," she said. "If you hadn't been so quick to react, there'd be no proof that Sophie lied and Madame wouldn't have got a confession out of her and... well, thank you."

"Whatever." Scarlett shrugged and looked down at her figure skates for a moment. Long blonde hair hid her face.

"Right then," said Frankie, when the other girl stayed silent. "I sort of need to get going—"

"You were pretty good out there..." mumbled Scarlett, biting her lip. "Well done."

Frankie nearly fell over. Scarlett Jones was congratulating her? She smiled. "Thank you. That means a lot—"

"I'll beat you next time, obviously," Scarlett interrupted.

"Yeah, of course," said Frankie. "Next time."

"Frankie!" called Dylan. "Do you want them to give your medal to someone else?"

With a final smile at Scarlett, Frankie skated away, her head held high and her heart bursting with pride. Only a short distance separated the barrier from the podium, where all the officials were waiting. Sophie LaFleur and Olga Krugalov were there already.

Sophie gave Frankie a sidelong glance. "Well done," she said, through gritted teeth.

But the Russian figure skater was more effusive in her praise. "You skated beautifully," said Olga, kissing Frankie on both cheeks. "You deserve gold."

"Thank you so much," said Frankie, shaking the Russian's hand.

Suddenly, the full impact of the moment hit Frankie and she found that she couldn't stop smiling. She, Frankie Wills, who had loved figure skating since she first stepped on the ice, and who had been glued to the television for every Winter Olympics, was actually here – *at* the Olympics – and about to be presented with *her very own gold medal.*

Someone tapped her on the shoulder.

Frankie spun round to see Madame von Berne. The coaching director had made her way across the ice and was smiling again as she pointed to someone hanging half over the barrier, cheering and clapping as if she'd never stop.

"Mum!" cried Frankie. Instantly, a lump rose in her throat and she found that she couldn't speak. Without a thought for the waiting officials, she skated towards her mum, tears of happiness coursing down her cheeks as she enveloped her in the biggest hug *ever*.

"Congratulations," Mum whispered in her ear. "You were unbelievable. Dad's thrilled too, of course. Josh says to tell you that they're all watching on the telly and to make sure your skirt isn't tucked in your pants when you get your medal." She squeezed her again. "You're a gold medallist, Frankie!"

Frankie smiled and wiped her eyes.

"Excuse me." It was Madame. "I think you might have to wind it up now…"

Quickly, Frankie said goodbye, promising to find Mum after the ceremony. She also promised to keep smiling, but there was no danger of her failing to do that. In fact, she wasn't sure if she'd ever be able to stop smiling again.

An Olympic official beckoned to Frankie and she joined Sophie and Olga behind the podium. The arena lights dimmed dramatically until only the spotlights focusing on the three medallists remained.

"And the winner of the Olympic Ladies' Figure Skating gold medal is…Frankie Wills!"

At last! It was the announcement that she had longed to hear her whole life. Filled with elation, Frankie stepped up onto the very highest level of the podium to the sound of deafening cheers from the many thousands of spectators. One by one, Sophie and Olga joined her, smiling and waving to the crowds.

The president of the International Olympic Committee stepped forward and placed the gold medal around Frankie's neck. She touched it gleefully, full of wonder at how *heavy* it was. The silver and bronze medals were awarded and then the National Anthem began to play…

Blinking back tears of happiness, Frankie gazed awestruck as three flags were ceremonially hoisted before them, the Union flag so much higher than the others, until they hung in the centre of the Olympic arena for all to see.

She'd done it.

She'd won gold.

And if Frankie thought she'd felt happy before this moment, it was nothing to the sheer joy she felt now, standing atop the podium as an Olympic gold medallist. Everything she'd gone through to reach this moment faded into the background. The endless hours of training, the spills, the obstacles… None of it mattered now.

As the last few notes of the National Anthem echoed around the stadium, Frankie smiled gratefully at Madame. "Thank you," she mouthed. Without Kristiana von Berne, she wouldn't be on this podium now. She would still be living at home, skating at the local rink. She wouldn't be an Olympic champion.

Madame smiled back. "Don't party too hard tonight," she called. "It's the World Figure Skating Championships next month. We've got to polish your routine for that."

Frankie grinned. She couldn't wait.

And then she looked across the ice for the one face that she really wanted to see right now. There he was, on the other side of the barrier. Dylan caught her eye and blew her a kiss. And then another. Frankie smiled back at him. She knew deep down that she'd be back here in two days' time, congratulating Dylan on *his* gold.

Frankie Wills smiled and smiled and smiled. It was no exaggeration to say that, right at that moment, she was the happiest girl in the entire world. She had a gold medal *and* an awesome boyfriend.

It really didn't get any better than this.

Catch up with the story so far...

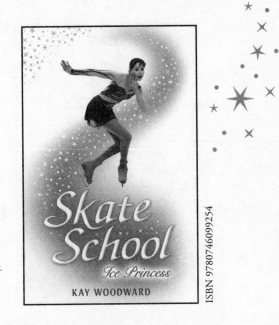

ISBN 9780746099254

Ice Princess

Frankie lives for her ice-skating, and has her
heart set on becoming a star. So it's a dream come
true when she's talent-spotted at her local ice rink
and whisked off to ultra-glam Skate School to
train for the Olympics.

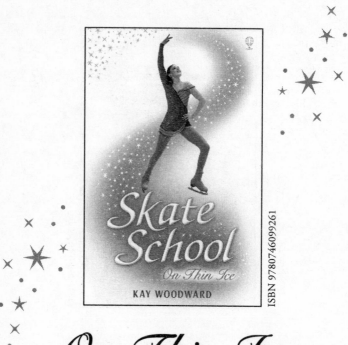

ISBN 9780746099261

On Thin Ice

Frankie's thrilled when she's chosen to skate with Paul in a high-profile competition. But Paul wants to skate alone. He wants to keep the spotlight – and the chance to win gold – to himself. It's a real problem when they're meant to be competing in Perfect Pairs. Together!

ISBN 9780746099285

Stars on Ice

Things are hotting up at Skate School and Frankie's
got her sights set on gold at the World Championships.
She's also falling for the gorgeous Dylan. The problem
is that any hint of romance is strictly forbidden by their
coach so Frankie and Dylan skate together in secret...

Look out for this sparkly new series about friendship and drama by Anne-Marie Conway.

"This book is fab."
Someone Important

Star Makers Club

Phoebe finds her Voice

Anne-Marie Conway

ISBN: 9781409516514

Can Phoebe solve all her problems and most of all overcome her stage fright in time to sing her musical solo?

Star Makers Club
STAGE

Polly plays her Part

"you'll LOVE this book!"

Anne-Marie Conway

ISBN: 9781409520917

With all the drama in her family, how can
Polly learn her lines in time for Star Makers'
fab new production?

CHECK OUT SAM'S
FABULOUSLY FUNNY STORIES
OF LIFE IN THE SPOTLIGHT...
FROM BEST-SELLING AUTHOR
KIMBERLY GREENE.

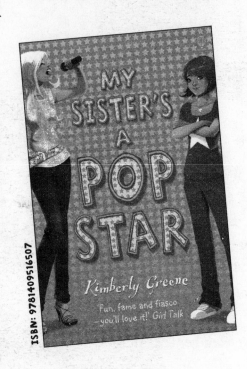

MY SISTER'S A POP STAR

Kimberly Greene

'Fun, fame and fiasco
—you'll love it!' Girl Talk

ISBN: 9781409516507

ISBN: 9781409524915

'FUN, FAME AND
FIASCO—YOU'LL
LOVE IT!'
GIRL TALK

ISBN: 9781409508298

For more sparkling reads,
check out
www.fiction.usborne.com